VAR

MINA CARTER
SUSAN HAYES

ABOUT THE BOOK

She'd do anything to find her daughter - even make a bargain with a beast.

Leia wants nothing to do with the aliens who invaded Earth. They're powerful, dangerous creatures who are a threat to every surviving human, especially women like her.

When alien raiders take her daughter, she's left with only one chance to see her again. Find one of the aliens and offer him a deal.

She never expected the beast she found would be the new Overseer's personal bodyguard. And she never imagined what would happen when she agreed to be claimed by an alien warrior named Var...

He came to this planet as a conqueror - only to find a female who brought him to his knees.

Var's orders were simple. Deal with a rogue warrior and protect the inhabitants of a human village. Then *she* ran into view...

Leia isn't like any female he's ever seen. She defies and confounds him, but there's no mistaking what she is... *his*.

This series contains hot, growly aliens on a mission to find their mates - and a group of women determined to free their planet... and themselves.

danger to shield them, they scurried out of sight as soon as they heard engines on the horizon or saw the disturbance in the air that indicated Tolath air-bikes on the move. Even a strange male voice was enough to scatter women with the genetic curse and those girls who were showing signs of it and send them into hiding.

Leia shivered as she hid in the darkness of a doorway and waited for the village square to empty of people. The sound of a familiar male voice on the other side of the square, near the village hall, had stopped her in her tracks. *B'rex*. He was the alpha that had "claimed" this area, including the village, as his personal kingdom. He didn't usually come here, but since his omega had died a week ago everyone had been on high alert as he stormed around, spouting the usual Tolath line about the betas "hiding what was owed."

Shit. She bit her lip as she pulled further back into the shadows.

If B'rex was here, she was in danger. She'd stopped taking her scent blockers a week ago, and if he caught a whiff of her scent she was done for. She'd never reach her goal—the exchange post outside of town.

Leia skirted carefully around the edges of the

1

OMEGAS STAYED HIDDEN. ALWAYS.

At least, that had been the creed Leia had lived by for the last twenty years. Ever since the Tolath had arrived and laid waste to Earth, she'd been on the run. Well, that wasn't entirely true. Only after the aliens had exploded their DNA bombs in the upper atmosphere and changed the human genome forever did people like her have to hide.

For twenty years she and other omegas had hidden themselves away, pretending to be betas any way they could. Between sticking to human-held villages and using herbs and other chemicals to disguise their omega scent, they'd managed to hide from the alien patrols and searches. With the help of the betas, many of whom put their own lives in village, making sure to stay downwind of B'rex. As she flitted between the buildings, she was forced to hide behind the flotsam and jetsam the villagers had scavenged from the old city just a few hours away.

She could barely remember the time "before" when she'd been free. When she'd been able to walk down the street at any time of day and take her daughter to the playground.

All that was gone. The cities of men were ruins destroyed by alien bombardment and age, the playground long gone. She rubbed her hand over the center of her chest. Even her daughter had been taken from her, rounded up in a surprise search.

She reached her goal at last, spying her target just outside the village—the trade post. It was why she was here. An omega in the open. Waiting for *them* to come and find her. She narrowed her eyes and studied the dirt flats around her, stretching as far as the eye could see in either direction. It didn't matter what she could see. They had cloaking technology. She wouldn't see them until they were right on top of her.

And then it would be over and the trap sprung. Gathering her courage, she broke from cover and ran. All she had to do was reach the exchange post...

He was alone, racing across the pockmarked wasteland beyond the walls of the citadel. For a few hours, he was free. Solitude was not something A'varen got to experience often. His duty didn't allow it. It was his honor to guard the Lord Overseer himself, a task that demanded all his skill, focus, and time.

Today, though, he was free from duty. His lord was spending the day in meetings with his most trusted advisors—men who would lay down their lives for him without hesitation should a threat arise. Not that they expected any. Zabor T'ah had not been breached since Lord Overseer Tane and his tribe had taken control of this planet recently. The xarthing human rebels had never dared to attack Zabor T'ah again. It would be suicide to try, and as insane as the rebels were, they did not die easily or without good cause. They were stubborn, ungrateful, and utterly confounding, but they were clever, too. He allowed himself a momentary weakness, an admission he would never make aloud. The humans leading the rebellion were too smart. That's why the lord was meeting with his men today. The L'crav should have tamed this world years ago, but the

Tolath who had conquered Earth had missed the differences in this race. They'd made mistakes and then compounded them with violence and cruelty.

The humans had fought back. Instead of a simple takeover where they claimed the omegas and established a breeding population, Earth had become a problem. The changes to the human's DNA had made them omegas, but there were too few of them, and they stayed hidden. Some whispered it had actually made the women more independent, but no one dared to say such a thing in the hearing of the Lord Overseer or any of the highblood.

He wasn't one of them, though. No royal blood ran in his veins. He'd fought his way through the ranks with his fists and his heart, proving himself worthy to be elevated—not to a position of power but to stand guard over those who wielded it.

His comms crackled, so he opened the line and spoke. "Var here."

"Where are you?" It was his kinsmen, A'rath.

"Out." He didn't get much time off, and he didn't want to be bothered today.

"I checked the locator on your air-bike. I know you're near Clearwater village. There's a problem."

He grimaced. This whole planet was a problem. "What is it?"

"One of the L'crav killed his omega last week, and he's causing trouble. Name's B'rex. The Lord Overseer asked me to handle it, but I've got another problem to deal with and can't leave right now."

A ball of fury burned in Var's gut. Omegas were to be protected. Only barbarians like the L'crav believed otherwise. It was why they had lost this planet. "Where is he?" he asked, his voice dropping to a growl that matched the engine of his air-bike.

"In the village. The village's leader claims this alpha believes they are hiding omegas and he's demanding they provide him with a new one. If that's true, he's in violation of Lord Tane's edict."

Xarth. "I'm on my way."

"Thought you'd say that. I'll be in touch once I've dealt with things here. Good hunting."

The village wasn't far. He'd deliberately avoided it because he wanted to be alone. Apparently the gods had other plans for him.

He barely slowed as he reached the outskirts of the village. It wasn't much more than a collection of huts huddled together in the middle of the wastelands. B'rex had to be wrong. Var couldn't imagine a delicate omega surviving in a place as harsh as this.

It was mid-afternoon. The center square should

be full of people, but only a handful of humans were in sight. They all wore drab grey clothes and kept their heads down as they scuttled away from the only source of noise in the village... the roar of an alpha.

As he stopped, a vision in red streaked out from between two buildings, her hair streaming behind her as she ran. Not ten paces behind her was B'rex, his face already contorted with the change. Eyes black, fangs dropped, his taloned hands reaching for the female in red.

The wind shifted then, and her scent hit him like a hammer blow to the chest. *Omega.* The roar burst from him before he could stop it, a bellow of challenge as he threw himself off the bike and gave chase. The change hit him between one step and the next, the sudden bulk of his bigger body tearing the seams of his jacket. But he didn't care. His black eyes fixed on the omega and the other alpha chasing her.

The barren landscape was nothing more than a blur as he ran. All he could see was his opponent as the other alpha reached out to grab the little omega. She screamed and threw herself sideways, the alpha's claws tearing her scarlet skirts before he overshot.

Var didn't give him the chance for another run at the female.

"*Mine!*" he snarled as he caught up, slamming broadside into the other alpha and taking him down to the dirt.

They tore at each other with fangs and claws, uttering howls of fury and challenge as they fought. B'rex raked his claws down Var's side. The pain was a distant thing that only spurred Var deeper into the change. Primal rage flowed through him and he drove his claws deep into the other male's body, the need to utterly destroy his rival fueling every blow.

The coppery tang of blood filled the air, and slowly the other male's challenges changed to cries of pain, and then to fear. With a twist and a vicious slash of his claws across Var's chest, he managed to wriggle free. Var slammed a hand down on his back, his claws raking vicious furrows as the male crawled on his belly to get away. Sensing his end at Var's hands, he was *fast,* getting away before Var could snatch him back. Rather than run, the wounds on his back evidence of his cowardice for all to see, he headed for the omega. Grabbing her, he shoved her between them—between two enraged males where she could be hurt, even killed.

Fury exploded through him. Var didn't stop. Didn't even slow down as he tore the omega away and went after the male in a flurry of claws and heavy blows. He didn't stop until the male beneath him was gone. He sat up, threw back his head, and roared his triumph to the empty sky.

Then, he caught her scent again, and he forgot about the male lying destroyed beneath him. He rose to his feet and turned to look at the human female. The omega. *His* omega.

2

Leia had screamed so much that no sound emerged now as the bloodied beast of an alpha turned toward her. Swallowing in fear, she backed away, trying to keep the ruined skirts of her dress covering her. Running was pointless. Alphas were mean and fast, as these two had just proven. She couldn't outrun them. Hell, she probably couldn't outrun them even on one of their air-bikes.

Huge. Terrible. Deadly. Bestial... Those were the words that filled her head as she got her first real look at the male in front of her. His all-black eyes gleamed with hunger and a terrifying intelligence she hadn't seen before. The other alphas had been animals. Cruel. Violent. Base. This male was... more. And that terrified her. He was big, even for an alpha, standing nearly seven feet tall in his current form—what the humans called beast mode. None of them understood the transformation, but they'd learned to fear it.

Dark hair, a jaw shadowed with stubble, and shoulders as broad as a building, he towered over her, blotting out the sun and sky.

Her hands clenched tightly in the skirts of her sundress, the only dress she owned and the prettiest thing she'd worn for years. Omegas didn't do pretty. They did *stay out of sight* and *don't call attention to themselves*. They wore mud streaked on their skin and hoods over their heads to hide. So being out in the open, in the red lace sundress, her dark hair brushed to a silken cape over her shoulders, the strands of grey hidden as best she could... it felt wrong. Sickeningly wrong.

He tracked her movements with those black-on-black eyes. But she couldn't run. It was too late. If she ran now, he would hunt her down like a wild animal. Taking a step to the side, she put her hand on the post embedded in the dirt at the side of the road. An exchange post, it was where bargains could be made and goods bartered. Where the Tolath sometimes traded goods or medicine for human items they couldn't get anywhere else.

Like an omega.

She just had to hope the beast-like alpha was in the mood to trade his help.

A growl rose from his chest. It was low and just on the edge of her hearing, but she heard it. Her knees weakened and the urge to run filled her again as her survival instincts kicked in. She locked her legs into place, knuckles white in the midst of her skirts. The other hand she kept flat on the warm metal of the post as she watched the alpha stalk toward her. A small whimper tried to work its way free of her throat, but she swallowed it back as he stopped in front of her.

He didn't move, just stood there, chest heaving as he looked down at her, dark eyes locked onto her. She didn't get much of a look at his face, just enough to register all the torn leather, piercing black eyes with no whites, and the darker lines that marked his chest like a tattoo... though she'd heard whispers they were born with those markings.

She didn't dare look for long. Humans did not look at the Tolath directly. It wasn't permitted. She bit back a small whimper of fear.

He held out his hand to her. "You are mine now. Tell me your name."

The deep rumble of his voice made her shiver,

the edge of that dangerous growl still in it. Some of the words were mangled by his growl but she could still understand him when he spoke in her language.

"My lord," she murmured, refusing to take his hand and shaking her head at the fact she was disagreeing with one of them. "I seek exchange by your laws."

He dropped his hand and inhaled again, leaning in to sniff along the side of her neck. "There will be no exchange. You are mine," he growled roughly. "You are an omega. *My* omega."

He made her jump when he moved. She tried to skitter sideways to get the post between them, but he had her hand, the strength in his terrifying. She risked a small glance up, finding him watching her with black eyes.

"I touched the post," she argued, her heart doing its best to break through her ribcage from pounding so hard. "By your species' law, I can request exchange."

At least, that was what she'd always been taught. Right now, though, she wasn't sure with her thoughts muddied by fear and the bloodied alpha looming over her. Her knees weakened, heat rolling through her as the need to agree to whatever he said filled her. Biting her lip, she ignored it, shaking her head and focusing on what she needed to do.

Looking up, she met his gaze directly. "Exchange. Please?"

"Tell me your name," he ordered, but his full lips twisted into the faintest hint of a satisfied smile. "Then you can tell me what you came here to exchange."

"Leia." Her voice was soft but she knew he'd heard. "My name is Leia. I need to find my daughter. She was..." She paused to collect herself. She knew better than to show fear to a predator. "She's an omega as well. She was caught in a raid a few weeks ago."

"You have an omega daughter? You have bred true already?" He studied her for long moments, and then his chest expanded.

"I am A'varen. Var to those I trust." He stood at full height and claimed his position with pride. "I am the shield of the Lord Overseer himself."

"*Nonono...*" She managed to snatch her hand from his, her eyes widening with panic.

She knew the name of the Overseer's Shield. A'varen was the stuff of legend and nightmare, said to have killed thousands with his bare hands when he'd arrived here. Women were rumored to have thrown themselves from the walls of the citadel rather than end up in his bed. She couldn't be claimed by the shield.

She'd expected to be found by a border guard or something, someone she could slip away from one night and make her escape once she'd found Savannah. But if he took her to the citadel, she would never escape. She would always be a slave and in the worst possible way—a slave to an alpha, forced to serve in his bed.

She backed away, shaking her head as she looked at him, her gaze flitting over his bloodied and torn leathers. Then her nerve finally broke... with a small cry, she grabbed her skirts and ran.

He roared and gave chase. Terror lent her feet wings and for one moment she thought she might actually do it. Then a hard arm caught her around the waist. "We were not done talking, little flower."

She cried out, struggling against his hold, but it was no good. His arm was like an iron bar around her waist and her feet didn't touch the ground. His chest was a steel plate against her back as she kicked out, losing her thin shoes in the process.

"No! Let me *go!*" she exclaimed, trying to get her fingers under the arm around her, but it was no good.

as they begged for their lives. Do not compare me or the H'thor to them again. If you do, I will punish you."

Her breath caught as fear flooded her system, but at the same time, his scent wound around her, a soft gasp falling from her lips as her traitorous body softened. Nonono, this couldn't be happening. She wouldn't respond to him... To cover up, she channeled her panic into anger.

"You're all the same!" she hissed. "Fucking aliens who took away everything!"

"Aliens. Yes. Fucking. *Soon*. Took away everything..." He paused but then smiled. "That's what conquerors do."

His fingers tightened on her shoulders as he pulled her in close and kissed her. There was nothing tender about it. He gave no quarter, his mouth as hot as a branding iron as it slanted across hers.

It was like kissing a mountain. He was all brute strength and muscle, but even as he took what he wanted, he didn't hurt her. His kisses were bruising but didn't bruise. His touch was hard but not painful.

She held herself still under the onslaught. Tried to... Against her wishes, against her fighting it, her body relaxed against his, her frame suddenly pliant. Squeezing her eyes shut, she concentrated on not responding, on letting him have what he wanted and no more. But even she couldn't control the shiver that rolled down her spine or the way her hands coiled in the fabric of his jacket.

He released her shoulder to bury the fingers of one hand in her hair, wrapping it around his fingers and then tugging her head back, baring her throat. He kissed his way from the corner of her mouth to her jaw and then along the side of her neck. Every kiss was hard, his fangs grazing her skin and leaving a trail of fire in his wake.

"Here," he murmured, sucking on her neck just above the pulse point. "That's where my mark is going to be. Showing everyone who you belong to."

She blinked, trying to marshal her thoughts, but they were scrambled, all disconnected. It took her a moment to collect herself, a feat that was near impossible with the hard heat of his body so close, and his lips brushing against her throat that way.

His mark. He would bite her.

The thought was like a bucket of cold water over her heated skin and she managed to get herself together enough to push at his shoulders. She put at least a little space between them.

"Will you help me find Savannah?" she asked, doggedly holding on to her original purpose.

He cupped her chin in one hand. "Your daughter? Her name is Savannah? Yes. I will find her. If she is dead... I will kill those responsible."

Relief filled her, even as she rejected the thought that Savannah might be dead. Gathering her courage, she reached up to touch his chest, the skin still streaked with blood, though the markings she'd seen earlier had faded now.

"Thank you," she whispered, dropping her gaze again to conceal the tears that blurred her vision.

"Look at me!" he snarled. "I am your alpha. If you want something, little flower, xarthing look at me when you ask."

3

Slowly, she looked up, the sweep of her dark lashes excruciatingly slow. Color painted her cheeks as her lips parted softly. Then her eyes met his and he couldn't look away. Lust slammed into him like a comet strike, burning away the last of his battle rage. His need for her was like a fire in his blood, a pain that wouldn't ease until he'd claimed her completely. He'd heard stories, but nothing had prepared him for the reality of this moment. Still, she was afraid of him. He could hear her heart racing from where he stood and smell her terror on her skin.

He gritted his teeth, ignored his aching balls, and tried not to think about what she'd look like bent over his bike, long legs bared, her pussy open to him as he... Shoving his lust-filled thoughts aside, he focused on the female in front of him.

Her emotions were all there in the forest green of her eyes—wariness and fear, relief and fledging hope, rounded out by resignation. She flinched when she saw his face and a tear rolled down her cheek. Something inside Var gave way and the change faded, his face resuming its normal shape with his fangs and claws retracting.

"All I ask is for you to help me find my daughter," she said in the softest voice he'd ever heard.

Her words touched a part of him he hadn't known existed. It evoked a new need... the need to comfort and soothe his female. He drank in the sight of her, seeing her clearly now that the haze of battle was gone. She was slender and poised, her stance reminding him of the highblood, a blending of elegance and command that couldn't be taught.

He moved without thinking, brushing away the errant tear from her cheek with a callused thumb. "Do you doubt my word? That is a punishable offense. Never question my honor."

He straightened and blew out a breath as if that could somehow clear her scent from his mind and help him think more clearly. It didn't. It couldn't.

Nothing would until he'd taken her to his bed and claimed her. And it had to happen soon, or their first time would be out here in this godsforsaken wasteland.

"Punishable?" she asked, a new sharp thread of fear entering her voice at the same time it tainted her delicious scent.

"Discipline of an omega falls to her alpha." His voice lowered to a growl. "Me. I will enjoy those sessions. And so, I think, will you. When I allow it."

She looked a little dazed as she reached out and took his hand. She slid her delicate fingers into his hold and let him turn her toward the bike. But, as focused as he was on her, he didn't miss the quick look around her. For a moment, his entire body tensed, ready to give chase.

"Don't run."

If she ran, he'd take her wherever they were when he caught her again. She deserved better than that. Godsblood, she deserved better than him. She knew that, of course. It was why she had questioned his honor. She knew he wasn't highblood. She doubted him. He clenched his jaw. He'd prove himself to her the way he'd done with everyone else.

With a small nod of her head, she let him guide her to the back of the bike but then stopped. The bike was built for his kind, not humans. She couldn't reach the seat.

With a growl in the back of his throat, he lifted her and deposited her on the back seat of his bike. The ruined skirt fell open, giving him a clear view of the length of one slender, silky leg, the skin far more delicate than his armored skin.

He ran a hand along her thigh, marveling at the softness of her skin. Her breath caught and she flinched away from him, nearly unseating herself in the process.

"Don't," he rumbled in warning. "You are mine. You will accept my touch."

She straightened up, shoulders squared, eyes straight ahead. "And if I don't?"

"Punishment."

Again, she tensed and shot him a sidelong glance. "You like that word."

"I like many things. You will learn them all in time." He moved his hand higher up her thigh, deliberately pushing the fabric aside to show more of her leg. "You are mine. Your body belongs to me."

She wanted to move away from him. He could tell. Her body tensed, the muscles in her thigh clenched as she forced herself to remain still. The scent of fear rolled from her as he leaned in.

Chapter 3

"You fear me." It wasn't a question. It was a statement. He was rewarded when she met his gaze for a second, the little intake of breath preceding her slight nod. What was it with these humans? Why did they fear their alphas so much?

Reaching out, he slid his hand into her hair, marveling at the softness of the silken strands. "Do not fear me. I am your alpha."

"That's exactly why I'm afraid of you," she muttered, her forest-green eyes blazing with intelligence for a brief moment before she dropped her gaze.

"I am your alpha. Why would you fear that?" He bit back a snarl of frustration and shook his head. "You will explain later. Now, I am taking us home."

He removed his hand and turned away from her. Taking a moment to adjust his straining cock to a more comfortable angle, he sat down in front of her and activated the bike.

They rose quickly. She uttered a soft squeak of fear and leaned forward to catch hold of his leathers, pressing herself against his back. Smiling to himself, he kept the bike a little off balance all the while, making sure she was forced to cling to him. He liked her touch. It eased the feral beast inside.

"Hold on," he said. Then they were racing across the wasteland, heading toward the black-walled citadel that was his home.

Zabor t'ah was four days' travel away for humans, a long and dangerous journey by one of the few trade convoys that ran through the wastelands. On a Tolath air-bike, though, that time was cut to less than a day.

He'd gone out today to escape from everything and bask in solitude. He'd thought that was what he needed. It wasn't. He needed Leia, her warm weight against his back. She'd fallen asleep, her omega instincts finally kicking in as she'd leaned against him. She knew. In her heart, she recognized him as her alpha. Now, he just needed to make her stubborn mind see the truth. He had some thoughts on how to do that… once they were alone.

"You're mine," he reassured her, pleased that she cleaved closer to him to avoid the stares of the others. He bared his teeth at any of his brothers who dared to look too long at his prize. He should have stopped to cover her lovely form before they entered, but he'd been focused on getting her back to his rooms before anyone realized he'd claimed an omega against the lord's standing orders.

By the time they reached the center of the tower, he was ready to do battle with anyone who dared to so much as look their way. His cock throbbed, his blood pounded in his ears, and his fingers gripped the handles of his bike so hard the metal had dented.

Once he had it parked in his stall, he twisted round to check on Leia. The scent of fear was on her again, and it tore at his senses. He dismounted, turned, and gathered her into his arms. A low rumble rose from his chest, surprising them both. He'd never made that sound before. It was the parth, the lovecall of an alpha to his omega, the way their kind expressed their adoration. In a sound, not words.

She curled up against his chest, not fighting him as he carried her through the corridors. Winding her arms around his neck, she seemed reassured by the low purring sound he made, and he caught the first hint of arousal rising from her body and wrapping itself around his senses like a caress.

But, much as he wanted to, he couldn't concentrate on that, not when every single one of his brothers turned to watch them pass, their nostrils flared. She was the first of her kind to be found since they'd landed.

An alpha took a step toward them and she squeaked, burying her face against the side of his strong neck. The way she curled against him made him want to roar in triumph. She was looking to him to protect her, which was as it should be. But then, J'tin made the foolish mistake of moving toward them, and the tiny omega squeaked in fear.

"Back off or you'll be shitting your teeth for a week," he growled at the foolish male in their own language.

J'tin stepped back but didn't stop staring. Nor did he move out of their way. "Where did you find her? Have you claimed this one?"

Var answered with a kick that took out the younger male's knee. He dropped to the ground, eyes wide, his mouth clamped shut to stop the sounds of pain. At least he was warrior enough to know better than to admit to pain.

Leia whimpered in distress and fear, and he began to parth again, trying to calm her. "I will protect you. That one will not look at you again. Do not fear, little flower. You are safe."

She relaxed against him a little and peeked around the strong column of his throat. None of the others were looking at her. They knew better after what had happened to J'tin.

"They won't?" she whispered. "Does that mean... you won't..."

She stopped talking abruptly, and a wave of frustration rolled through him.

"I won't what?" He stopped and looked down at her. "If the presence of these others worries you, don't let it. My rooms are not far away."

She stayed quiet. He assumed he'd been right. The presence of the other males had her unwilling to speak. The door to his room unlocked as he approached, the bracer on his wrist notifying the system of his presence. Once the door closed behind them, his tension eased, only to be hit broadside by a fresh surge of lust for the female in his arms.

"You're safe, now. Welcome home, little flower."

4

Leia didn't move, still held in his arms against his broad chest as she looked around the rooms. They were larger and more luxurious than anything she'd ever seen, even in her memories of before the Tolath had arrived, and for a moment she was speechless.

Plush, warm-looking rugs covered cool marble tile with elegant sofas and large windows to let in the light. It was everything she'd thought a palace should look like. Through the far door, she could just see a bedroom, and she looked away quickly.

"Do you... you live alone?" she asked quietly, not sensing anyone else in the rooms. It was a skill all omegas learned early, along with the ability to hide and breathe as soundlessly as possible.

"I am the Shield of my Lord," he said with pride. "As such, I have my own rooms close to his lord's, so that I am always nearby. No one else will disturb you here. I will see to it that only female servants are allowed access."

He walked over to the window with her still in his arms. The view was stunning, the streets of the citadel running straight and true up to the walls that guarded this place and those inside. Inside we green parks and flowers, a stark contrast to the barr lands beyond the gate. He nodded to the view. "Behave and I will take you out there and show you every part of your new home. It is a good place."

Her eyes widened in wonder at the view and the parks.

"I haven't seen a park for years," she admitted in a low voice. He hadn't put her down yet and all of a sudden, being so close to him was overwhelming. She struggled against him, pushing against his shoulders until he released her. As soon as her feet touched the floor, she backed up, putting distance between them and watching him, not the view.

"Why do you fear me?" he demanded, his voice rough and low. Again, he started to make that rhythmic, growling sound.

He was angry and she had nowhere to go,

nowhere to hide. So she backed up against the window, watching him warily. "You're an alpha," she said, trying to keep her voice level.

She was exhausted. The short nap on the back of A'varen's bike had not been enough to make up for the days of travel to get to the village with the exchange post, a dangerous journey for a woman anyway, omega or not... but she knew it was even more deep-rooted than that.

The curse in her DNA hadn't just rendered her a mere plaything, a breeder for the first Tolath alpha to find her. It had done more. It had altered her on a base level and in ways the hidden omega community were still discovering. There were the physical symptoms, the need that clawed at them as though it wanted to consume them from the inside out once a year—twice if they were as unlucky as she was—and everything that came with that. But it had also made them more delicate and as liable to be preyed on by the few human men left as Tolath alphas.

In the last couple of years, the tiredness had gotten worse. The bone-numbing exhaustion left her vulnerable. The few doctors they had theorized it was because omegas *needed* to submit to alphas. Without that link they would weaken and eventually die. The longer an omega went without an alpha, the worse the effects.

Only her fear kept her on her feet and watching him.

"I am *your* alpha. The moment I caught your scent, I knew you were mine." He scrubbed a hand through his short hair. "You aren't like the others I've met. They weren't mine. You are."

He tapped a massive fist to his chest. "I *parth* for you. That has never happened before."

She frowned, trying to process everything. He hadn't moved toward her as she'd expected, staying a couple of steps away and watching her with that dark gaze.

"Parth? That's what that sound is?" she asked, taking a step to the side followed by another.

He didn't stop her, moving parallel but staying the same distance away. Keeping an eye on him, she moved away from the window, skirting around the furniture as she explored the main room. She couldn't stop touching things, reveling in the plush furnishings. They were like nothing she'd ever seen, a tactile delight, but she made sure to stay away from the door to the bedroom. Well away.

"It is the sound an alpha makes when he has found his omega. It is a sign of..." he frowned and waved a hand. "Affection? Is that the word you humans use? There is no translation in my language."

There was nowhere to hide. No bolthole she could see that she could barricade against him. Most omegas learned to find small spaces to hide in during the day, out of sight, away from roving alpha patrols, and they'd hidden for so long it was second nature to her now.

"Affection?" she asked in surprise, pausing with her hand on the softest blanket she'd ever felt over the back of one of the sofas. The temptation to pick it up and wrap herself in it assaulted her. "You feel affection for me?"

"You are my omega," he said, as if that explained everything. "No other female will ever draw the parth from me. When I claim you, my cock will swell and knot." He smiled, a wicked gleam in his eyes. "I look forward to experiencing that."

Her breathing caught in her throat, ice rolling down her spine. She'd heard horror stories of the alphas' knots. They all had. About how it hurt when it swelled and tore when the alpha decided to continue. She'd seen the damage they caused, nursing the few who had survived breeding.

She couldn't do this.

Casting a look at the nearest door, the one to the corridor, she bolted. Heart thundering in her ears, she managed to get through it, his roar filling the air behind her. The first door off the corridor was locked, refusing to open even when she shoved at it, so she moved on, racing down to check the next one. It was open... but a bedroom.

Hearing heavy steps behind her, she realized she didn't have a choice and raced through it. With a strength she didn't know she had, she toppled a dresser to block the door and looked around wildly. Desperate, she yanked the ventilation panel off the wall. The space was small but she might be able to wriggle in.

She didn't even try. Hearing a loud crash at the door, she raced for the closet and yanked it open. She found a tiny crawl space at the back and tucked herself in under a blanket. Trying her best not to breathe, she counted slowly. All she had to do was wait for him to think she was in the ventilation shafts and then escape.

Somehow.

~

She'd run from him. Again.

Chapter 4

He'd let her explore as much as he was able, trying to give her a chance to adjust to her new reality. She touched everything, and he felt a spike of white-hot jealousy every time her hand caressed something that wasn't him. She liked soft things, he noted. And she moved so quietly, like prey hiding from the hunter. *Him.*

But when she ran... his control shattered and he gave in to the instincts. He gave chase, the feral part of him rejoicing in the chance to go on the hunt.

When she ran into one of the spare rooms, he grinned as the door slammed shut behind her. There was no way out. No door was going to keep him from his prize. She had a lot to learn about alphas if she thought that would help.

He heard a crash and grinned to himself, his jaw aching with the need to drop his fangs. She was barricading herself in. Clever little omega. But she seemed to have forgotten where she was. This was his territory, and here, he ruled absolute.

He tested the door. It didn't move. So he backed up and hit it with the full weight of his body. It moved.

"Something you should know, little flower," he growled by the door, knowing she could hear. "It isn't wise to run from your alpha. We're hunters. We like to chase."

He hit the door again and whatever she'd used to barricade it moved again. Another hit, and he was able to shove his way through the gap.

He saw the ventilation shaft pried open and his heart skipped a beat. Surely she hadn't gone that way. The danger... He raced over, inhaling and checking for her scent. No. It wasn't strong enough for her to have gone that way.

He turned and looked around the room, letting his nose and instincts guide him. "I'm glad you didn't try to escape that way. You could have been hurt."

He stalked toward the bed, trying to isolate where she was. In the middle of the room, he caught a trace of her scent. It was coming from the far side of the room.

The closet.

He strode over and yanked the door open, letting the light fall into the darkness. Where was she? He crouched down, trying to catch a glimpse of his prize in the cramped and cluttered space. "Come out. Now."

Silence met his demand. He glared into the dark space, waiting. He didn't reach in. The scent of her terror was too thick, and she might hurt herself in the close confines. But he didn't have to wait long. Bursting from her hiding space, she barreled into him, trying to knock him over and rush past him.

He grunted in surprise but didn't move. Appearing dazed from the impact, she moved too slowly to escape when he wrapped her in his arms, locking her to him before letting himself fall backward so she was sprawled across his massive frame.

He held her tightly, pinning her body full length against him as she squirmed and fought to get free. "There's nowhere for you to go. You offered yourself. I agreed to your terms. You are mine, by my agreement and your own."

All the fight went out of her in a heartbeat and she collapsed against him, a tremble running through her tiny frame. She rested her forehead against his shoulder, her words soft and pleading. "Please... don't hurt me."

"Never."

He touched her face, his callused fingers gentle as they traced the line of her jaw. "You are a gift. A treasure." He grimaced. "I am not good with pretty words, but you are all of that and more. I don't understand. Why are you so afraid?"

She opened her eyes to look at him and the expression there made him cold to his soul.

"When the Tolath first arrived, the bombs made us sick and some of us died. Savannah and I were both ill and I was terrified she'd die. Then the patrols came..." her voice dropped to a haunted whisper. "The alphas came, sweeping through the towns one night. We didn't realize we'd been changed to omegas." Hatred dripped from the word, making him wince.

"But it wasn't enough to have turned us into sexual playthings. The alphas were brutal and terrifying, moving from woman to woman, never satisfied." Her voice changed and became flat, unemotional, like she was recounting something from a book. "Those caught in the open were raped repeatedly. Knotted and torn when the alpha didn't get the satisfaction they expected. Most didn't survive the night."

For a moment he couldn't move, trying to make sense of her words. Then he swore, low and venomous.

"The L'crav. Those animals. May their leaders scream out their torments forever in the dark." The muscles in his jaw clenched, and an anger as hot as the sun burned in his veins. "I killed them too quickly. They did not deserve my lord's mercy."

He cupped her face. "Did they hurt you?" he demanded, unable to keep the harshness out of his voice. "Tell me and I will purge every last one of them from existence."

She shivered and closed her eyes. He wasn't as naive to think it was from pleasure at his touch. She was still terrified, and it seemed, with good reason. "No." She shook her head, refusing to look at him. Her throat moved as she swallowed. "I hid with Savannah. Kept us both out of sight."

"Your daughter is older than I imagined and you are braver than I expected from one of your kind. To protect your daughter that way... alone." He raised his head and kissed her as gently as he was capable of. "I should have been there for you both."

She didn't respond, not at first, but she didn't pull away, letting him kiss her. Triumph filled him. Unlike the first kiss he'd given her, he was more in control now. Now he had her secured and in his lair, he could concentrate on learning the shape of her lips with his own.

He kept his hand on her cheek as he kissed her and then slowly slid it into her hair. His entire frame taut, he made sure to keep his touch gentle. His tongue swept into her mouth, his hand tightening on her hair just enough to hold her still as he tasted and teased with a focus straight from his feral side. He needed to know the taste of her and what her surrender felt like.

Her hands spread over his upper chest for balance, and his parth deepened.

Her fingertips brushed the bare skin exposed by the neck of his shirt and she snatched them away like she'd been burned. He growled in irritation and deepened the kiss to distract her. He was sure she didn't notice her fingertips returning. She whimpered, a soft sound in the back of her throat as he turned them, bracing himself above her as she lay on the soft carpet.

He called again, the low rumble deeper. He could have crushed her with his weight, but he held himself off her with the strength of his arms, his biceps bulging, forearms tensed as he kissed her again and again.

5

Var felt the tremors running through her delicate frame, and no alpha could miss the scent of her fear on the air. So he kept things light, teasing and tempting her rather than crushing her lips beneath his in demand. All the while he called to her, and before long, he felt her relax. Just a little, but it was enough. He didn't want her fear. He craved her surrender instead. She broke from the kiss to look at him in surprise. "You are not what I expected."

The smile he gave her was warmer this time. "Neither are you, little flower."

He dropped his head and kissed her again, but before she could react, he pushed himself off her, rising to his feet. Then he leaned down and offered her his hand.

"Come. You will never, never have to be afraid again."

She sat up, watching him. He couldn't read the expression on her beautiful face and frustration rolled through him. She needed to trust him. He was her alpha. But she wasn't running anymore, so that was something. She'd let him kiss her, claim her mouth, but he wanted far more. Her gaze flickered from his hand to his face and back again. It was all he could do to hold still and let her think she was making the decision.

Slowly, she reached up to slide those delicate little fingers into his grip.

He felt the same as he did when he'd been entrusted with the life of his lord. He closed his hand around hers and lifted her to her feet, noting again how graceful she was but also how little she weighed. He would see to it she had all the best foods to choose from. She would not go hungry again.

He looked down at her filthy, bare feet. She needed shoes, too. And clothes. But there was time for that later. Much, much later. He swept her into his arms again and walked out of the room, heading straight for the one place he needed to be right now.

His bed.

Chapter 5

The door to his room was already open, the sheets turned down by one of the palace servants while he'd been away.

He set her down on the edge of the bed, mildly amused to note her feet dangled over the edge far above the floor. "This is my room. You will sleep here, with me."

He shrugged out of the sleeveless overcoat and tossed it onto a nearby chair. Then, he pointed to the wall laden with weapons. "You will not touch those. You do not know how to use them, and most of them will only work with my DNA. You could be hurt if you disobey me on this. Do you understand?"

Her eyes widened and she nodded, eyeing the wall warily as if the weapons would somehow leap from their brackets and assault her. "I never learned to fight," she said in a soft voice. "Just to hide and to run."

"Which you did successfully for many years." He removed his gun belt next, hanging it on a hook beside his other weapons. "You can be proud of that. Given how the L'crav behaved, it was all you could do." Just thinking about the other clan triggered a surge of anger. Clenching his jaw, he had to remind himself to relax before he scared her again.

Beneath the jacket he wore a sleeveless shirt whose sole purpose was to stop the leather sticking to his skin. Stripping it off, he turned back to face her, letting her see him properly. He was the biggest of his clan, a warrior she would be proud of.

Her breathing caught as she looked at him and he saw the struggle in her eyes. The need to bolt off the bed was evident in the tense lines of her delicate frame, but then she lifted her chin and met his eyes. He saw the effort it cost her to stay in place, her knuckles white as she gripped the sheets on either side of her hips. He watched her gaze waver and then flit over his body, almost unwillingly. But the way her eyes darkened got to him the most, drawing his parth from him again.

Stalking over to the bed, he didn't stop until his thighs were pressed against her knees.

"I will never hurt you." He tapped his fist to his chest. "I swear to it. I am not like the others. We are nothing like them. They were dishonorable, belly-crawling snakes. I am H'thor. It means honor."

He thumped his hand to his chest again, fighting to find the words to express himself. "I get no joy from seeing your fear. So stop it."

She tilted her head slightly to the side. "You don't know much about humans. Do you?"

His brain locked as he tried to listen to her instead of stare at the rise of her breasts or the way she bared her throat as she tilted her head. "I... no. We haven't been on this planet long. What did I get wrong?"

The smile she favored him with was small but spellbinding. "You can't just tell me to stop being afraid. It doesn't work that way."

He huffed in frustration. "It should. You should listen to everything I say and obey me. Every other race we've conquered, that's the way of it. But not you humans. You are different." He set his hands down over hers and leaned in until their mouths were a scant breath apart. "And oh, so stubborn."

She didn't move away from him or shrink back. Her eyes reflected the darkened forest as she looked back at him.

"That's just women," she told him in a soft voice. "My dad always said my mom was the most difficult woman he'd ever met."

"Before you were changed, all females were like this?" He tried to imagine what that must have been like, but his imagination failed him. "How did the males get anything done?"

She gave a soft laugh. Instantly it became his favorite sound in the world. "Mom said they just needed to learn to do as they were told and everything would be okay."

"Do as they were told?" he snorted. "No wonder we conquered this planet so easily. At least, the males were conquered. But the females..." He gave in to temptation and reached up to twine a lock of her hair around his fingers. He liked the soft weight of it, with strands of grey that lightened the color and spoke of her strength and will to survive. "Later, you are going to tell me more. Especially about the females."

"Later?" she asked and then caught her breath. "*Oh...*"

"Much later." He leaned in and kissed her, his free hand leaving hers to slide up her thigh, taking her torn dress with it. She was so small his hand spanned the top of her leg easily, but her skin was soft and the scent of her arousal was impossible to ignore.

"Lovely. All the males in the citadel will envy what I have." But no one would envy him the task of explaining to his lord that he had broken the edict on claiming omegas. That... was tomorrow's problem.

She stiffened beneath his hands. "Others. Like, in the hallway? You... you won't share me. Will you? Please don't share me."

"Share you?" Appalled, he spat the words. "Never! You are mine, Leia. You will never know another cock but mine. I do *not* share. Your children will be mine. If you look at another male, I will kill him. If you touch another male, I will kill him *and* his family, and you will be punished. You will not enjoy that punishment."

She made a small, instinctive move toward him, her fingers against his lips and distress on her beautiful face.

"No... please? I won't." She gave a small sound that could be a laugh. "Most omegas won't even look at or touch human men, never mind alphas."

He opened his mouth and kissed her soft fingertips. "I am my Lord's Shield. Killing those who threaten him is my duty. But... I will not kill anyone who looks at you." He winked. "But only because you asked nicely. If they touch you? They die."

She nodded, pulling her hand back more slowly this time. She looked spellbound, so close to him he could feel the heat of her skin against his. The tension and fear he'd sensed before were duller now and fading. And she'd touched him. Willingly. He wanted her to touch him more.

He traced a finger around the curve of her ear and then let it wander down the lines of her neck to the place where her red lace strap crossed over her shoulder.

"I am *your* alpha. You will touch me." He dropped his mouth to her skin, following the path of his finger a moment before.

6

For a moment she was still, years of fear and horrific stories holding her prisoner. He wasn't those alphas from that night, though. He was different. She'd been in his company for hours and he hadn't hurt her. If he'd been like the other alphas, he would have taken her in the blood-soaked dust by the exchange post.

She bit her lip at the feel of his lips brushing her ear and then her neck as he worked his way down to her shoulder. Hesitantly, her hand came up to his shoulder, the skin hot beneath her fingers. The world didn't end, and he didn't turn into a ravening beast so she smoothed her hand over him. Exploring.

His muscles flexed under her fingers in an instinctive show of strength. Scars spanned his chest and arms—so many she couldn't count them all. They were a reminder that he was a creature of violence, but she was starting to believe that perhaps he wasn't a threat to her.

He moved his hand, sweeping the strap of her dress off her shoulder to fall limply against her upper arm. His hand kept going, sliding down her arm to her wrist and then up her ribcage to cup her breast through the thin fabric.

Her small gasp was near silent, just a catch of breath, but she knew he'd heard it because he started to make that strange rumbling sound again, almost like a purr. This time, though, the sound was harder-edged, less soothing. Instead, it sparked heat low in her belly and she shifted position on the bed, arching against him.

He hissed something in his guttural tongue and stroked her nipple in hard, tight circles. She shivered with pleasure and then gasped in shock as he tore open her dress baring her breasts with a short, hard movement of his hands. Bowing his head, he replaced his fingers with his lips. He drew her into the hungry heat of his mouth, laving her tender nipple with the tip of his tongue.

Thought was impossible, her body pliant under his hands. Heat arced through her, from her nipple directly to her clit. She pressed her thighs together, trying to ease the sudden, savage ache there. It was like the curse... but didn't feel wrong. There was no panic or confusion. Instead, she slid her hand up the back of his neck, driving her fingers into the short strands of his hair to hold him to her.

He devoured her with a single-minded focus, battering down what little resistance she could muster. He moved from one breast to the other, coaxing her body to respond to him in ways she couldn't have imagined.

He tore away more of her dress, reducing it to tatters with breathtaking ease. Raising his head, he smiled at her with a predator's grin that made her heart race. Without a word, he placed one massive hand between her breasts and pressed her backward onto a bed so big she could have curled up in one corner.

"Need to taste you."

She surrendered to the movement and lay back against the sheets. They were so smooth and soft against her skin that at any other time she'd have luxuriated in the sensation, arching like a cat to rub herself against them.

But not now. Now, all she could see was him over her and the demand in his black-on-black eyes as he looked down at her. The shiver that hit her was less to do with the temperature in the room and more the heat that swept over her skin and charged through her veins. Her nipples were hard buds, aching for more of his touch as her clit throbbed in response.

She'd spent so many years hiding that this felt odd. Letting a man, an alpha, look upon her naked form, only a small pair of panties hiding her pussy from him, was... Her arms moved instinctively to cover herself up. The growl that exploded through the silence was low and dangerous. His black-on-black eyes flashed with something but it was gone before she could identify it.

"Don't," he warned, "or I will punish you."

It was the fourth time he'd mentioned punishment but the first time the word hadn't caused a cascade of panic to tumble through her. Instead, her cheeks colored as anticipation rolled through her, a rush of wet heat dampening her panties. She closed her eyes, hiding herself from him the only way she could. She couldn't be turned on by that idea, surely? Only this morning she'd been terrified of him touching her, of what he would do to her...

Var inhaled slowly, teeth flashing white against the dark frame of his beard. "Yes."

Chapter 6

He moved slowly, callused hands gliding across her overheated skin. Everything felt too real, too much. Need flooded her mind and she arched her hips off the bed as he drew her wet panties down her hips and along her legs.

When they were off, he raised them to his mouth and breathed in so deeply she could see his chest rise like a bellows. "Mine."

She bit her lip. He still had one large hand wrapped around her ankle, his callused palm abrading her delicate skin. Instead of trying to pull free from his hold, she arched her back, her hands in her hair as she showed off for him.

He tossed the scrap of fabric aside in an instant, his eyes locked on her. His grip shifted on her ankle, raising her leg and sliding it over one bare shoulder as he prowled forward, his gaze never wavering as he settled his big body between her legs.

She lay exposed and vulnerable in a way that should have terrified her, but she was past fear now. Something else had taken hold, stronger than fear but just as powerful. Need.

He turned his head and pressed an open-mouthed kiss to her inner thigh. Then he worked his way higher, not stopping until his mouth found the seam of her pussy, his tongue stroking along the edge once, twice, and then...

She arched off the bed as he pressed his face into her folds, going straight for her throbbing clit. Her small cry was loud in the silence of the room, and she grabbed for the bedding, mangling the silken sheets in her hands. He didn't let up, devouring her with an intensity and focus she couldn't process. He seemed to take the tiny movement of her hips as an attempt to get away from him, and a growl erupted from his chest, vibrating against her as his large hands closed over her hips, holding her in place.

The growl mixed with the deeper thrum of his lovecall, the vibration buzzing against her clit with explosive results. Her senses scattered to the four winds as an orgasm started to build, stealing her breath and making it impossible to think about anything but the sensations he was unleashing on her with his mouth and tongue.

Everything in the world faded away, leaving her with nothing to cling to but him. His breath warmed her skin. His touch. The branding heat of his mouth. The strength in his hands. She could feel it all so intensely, and it all felt right.

A sob escaped her at the pleasure, without the pain she was used to from suffering through her heat

Chapter 6

alone for so many years. With a ragged gasp, she turned her head, trying to hide her tears from him as she rode out the waves of bliss.

He growled as he gave her a last lick, the heated lash of his tongue making her yelp and her hips come off the bed. Then he was over her again, his eyes narrowed and dark as he turned her head so she had to look at him.

He wore an expression of pure male satisfaction as he stared down at her. His lips gleamed with the proof of her arousal as he lowered himself to kiss away her tears. She shuddered in reaction as his lips brushed her skin. He didn't comment, but he didn't stop until every tear was gone. Then he shifted, rocking his weight onto one arm in a display of strength that was both terrifying and fascinating as he reached between them to tear open his pants.

She dared to raise her head, needing to look. She had to know if the rumors were true. They were. He was huge, and she couldn't even see all of him.

"How?" she whispered as a flicker of fear managed to break through her desire-addled mind.

He moved over her, hands beside her shoulders, his eyes staring down at her. "Don't panic, little flower. I will never hurt you."

Then he rocked his hips, letting the wide crown

of his cock stroke over her folds. Her hips jerked in reaction, the touch almost too much against her oversensitive flesh. Pinned between him and the bed, she couldn't go far and that brief touch sparked a chain reaction of need again. Her soft moan preceded a rush of wet heat that bathed the head of his cock. He stroked over her folds again, each pass making the hardened length of him slick, slippery with the evidence of her need.

Desire built until she panted, hands fisted and hips moving in time to his light thrusts. He dropped his head to kiss her, his tongue invading her mouth as he changed the angle of his next pass, pressing himself into her channel.

She expected there to be pain and had steeled herself for it. Sex wasn't fun for omegas. It was cruel and terrifying... all about the alpha's pleasure. All an omega could hope for was to satisfy the alpha quickly and pray it was over soon. Most pain could be endured if it was quick.

But there was no pain—only a faint twinge as her body gave way to his. He groaned, a wild sound that was nowhere near human. She felt every ridge of his cock as he slid into her. She'd heard they were built that way but had never seen for herself. Never wanted to see. Until now.

Chapter 6

He didn't stop until he was buried to the hilt inside her, her body impossibly full. Every throb and twitch sent a fresh surge of cream to bathe his cock. He didn't stop kissing her, stroking his tongue against hers in an erotic demand. She tasted herself on him, and that sent her arousal higher.

He hadn't just taken her roughly and without care. He'd brought her to soul-shattering pleasure first. Made her slick and wet enough to take him without pain. Even now, even as he throbbed within her, he wasn't pounding her into the mattress as she'd been told an alpha would. Instead, he held himself still, tension running through his massive frame, as though he was waiting for something.

She didn't know what it was at first, but then, in a moment of clarity she understood. He was waiting for her.

She closed her eyes and, for the first time in her life, let herself give in to the needs that tore through her. Arching beneath him, fingers tightening in his hair, she tentatively kissed him back.

He shuddered, growled, and began to move over her. Every stroke of his hips pinned her to the mattress, every movement filling her, rubbing over nerve endings she didn't know she had. It was like falling into fire, and she let it consume her.

7

Her surrender was so sweet, Var almost lost control then and there. Her soft lips moved against his, her kiss wary and seeking. It was all he could do not to crush her mouth with his and take control.

He held on, even though the fire of need raged within him and demanded that he pin her down to take what he wanted. What was his by right. But his little omega was only just beginning to trust him, so he kissed her back. He allowed her to lead their kiss but controlled his possession of her body with long strokes. She whimpered and clenched around him.

He could still taste her, a nectar as sweet as sun-ripened fruit and as intoxicating as the homebrew they served in his favorite bar. The more she gave herself up to him, the harder it was not to lose control. He fought it, determined to bring her to release again before that happened.

He needed to show her the rewards of surrender. Make her want *him*.

Her body milked his cock, the heat and pressure drawing another growl from deep in his chest. His omega was beautiful. Perfect.

"*Mine*," he tore his mouth from hers to press his lips to her throat, feeling her pulse flutter beneath the silken skin. He didn't hesitate before he bit down, letting her blood spill over his tongue. She arched beneath him, crying out in shock and sudden, explosive release.

Her tiny body, already almost too tight for the thickness of his cock, clamped down around him hard and he growled, low and feral. Limp with pleasure, a low moan escaped her lips as he sped up, fucking her through her release and right into another. When he pulled back, her eyes were wide and dark... almost fully blown in the mating heat. Just like his.

Satisfied, he pulled her closer, his arms like steel bands around the back of her hips, lifting her higher as he chased his own release.

She was so tight he felt every ridge slide into her

heat, her body so responsive he felt like he could stay like this forever, fucking her until they both collapsed into exhausted slumber. His body, though, wanted more than that. It wanted the one thing it had never had. The base of his cock began to swell, balls tightening. He emptied himself inside her with hard, shaking thrusts that slowed only when his knot formed, locking them together in a bond so tight he had to grit his teeth against the pleasure of it.

He braced himself over her to avoid crushing her slender body beneath his weight but his arms shook with the intensity. She moaned in pleasure... he imprinted the soft sounds on his memory. The noise his little flower made the first time she felt his knot.

Coming back to himself, he moved to brush her hair back from her face, planting soft kisses against her nose and her cheeks as he called softly to her again. The sound was low and meant to comfort. She looked up at him, the black of her eyes receding so he could see the beautiful color again. Disappointment rolled through him. She was not in mating heat.

Her stunning green eyes went wide with panic, and her body tensed around him to the point of pain as she registered his knot.

His parth intensified, but it wasn't enough. "Shhh. I know. It is..." He bowed his head to hers, kissing her softly and trying to distract her from her fear. When she exhaled, he nuzzled her cheek, feeling the tension leave her body. Rocking his hips against her, just a little, he drew a soft gasp of pleasure from her lips.

"Mine now."

Movement wasn't possible, just tiny rolls of his hips that would pull gently on the knot, allowing him to grind his pelvis against hers and trap her clit between them. Each time, she shivered and bathed his cock in another delicious rush of heat.

"See, little flower?" He nuzzled under her ear. "You have nothing to fear."

Her tiny sounds of pleasure were music to his ears. She was so responsive, so addictive.

She stirred, her expression still dazed and her eyes cloudy with passion. "You're so big."

"I am." He rocked his hips again in a gentle tug. "But you were made for me."

A ghost of a smile touched the corners of her mouth. "Arrogant man."

He liked her smile. He wanted to see more of it.

"Arrogant alpha," he corrected her.

"Pfft," she made a dismissive gesture with her hand, wrinkling her nose. He gaped for a moment. Was she sassing him? Not a wise move, not when he was buried balls deep inside her, his knot swollen to lock her to him.

He wrapped his arms around her and turned onto his back, taking her with him but careful not to let their bodies move too far apart.

She squeaked in surprise, staring down at him from her new position.

"Who do you belong to, little omega?" he demanded, keeping one arm locked around her as his other toyed with her hair again. He loved her hair. She would not cut it again.

That little smile flirted with the corner of her lips again. "Well..."

She tilted her head, lips pursed, the movement only halted by his hold in her hair. He growled in warning. His name should be the first thing on her lips.

"Who. Do. You. Belong. To?" He bit out the words.

He didn't know if he was proud or pissed when she waited half a heartbeat before answering him. "You."

He brought his hand down on her ass, not hard enough to hurt, but the message was clear. "If anyone asks you that question, you will not hesitate. You belong to A'varen of the H'thor."

She spread her hands out over his chest, tracing the lines of his scars with delicate fingers.

"I belong to..." she paused and then frowned. "Well dammit, I forgot."

"No forgetting!"

This time, his hand came down harder, the satisfying smack of flesh on flesh making her jump. A spike of need tore through him as her body tightened around his knot. He had to fight for breath.

By the time he was in control again, she was smiling broadly, her eyes dancing with that same wicked intelligence he'd seen before.

"You..." He blew out a ragged breath. "Xarth. Why are you so stubborn?"

Her smile slipped a little at his words, a tiny frown appearing in the center of her brow.

"I'm sorry," she said quickly, leaning forward to press against him. "I was only teas... what the hell is that?"

She broke off at the soft sound breaking up her words, her hand flying to her throat. Her gaze lifted to his, her confusion utterly adorable as the sound deepened with each breath.

Her parth was as beautiful as she was, calling to a part of him that had always been alone. It entranced him, and before he knew it, he had her folded into his arms, her head cradled against his chest as he rumbled in response. His knot softened as he held her, wrapped up in a sense of peace he'd never known before.

"That is your parth, my omega." He couldn't keep the pride from his voice. "Your true nature is manifesting. You have accepted me."

She uttered something that was part laugh, part groan, her words muffled against his skin as she continued to parth. "You don't have to sound so smug about it."

"Oh yes, little flower. I do."

8

Since the moment she'd met A'varen, Leia's life had become a series of nonstop changes and surprises. Nothing had gone the way she'd expected, but the most surprising thing of all was when Var had kissed her forehead and told her he'd be back soon. Then he left her alone and unguarded in his rooms.

At first, she thought it was a test. That he'd be back any second to try and catch her out. But he hadn't. He'd left most of his weapons on the wall, including several wicked-looking knives.

He'd ordered enough food and drink to feed half the citadel. Some of the simpler items came from the machines in what passed for a Tolathian kitchen while other, more elaborate dishes were brought in by betas who performed their tasks without comment.

She smiled and said hello, but they ignored her, barely even looking her way before leaving. Biting her lip she approached the food, eyeing up the unfamiliar dishes. Her stomach had been empty since... she frowned and rubbed at it. Actually, she couldn't remember the last time she ate. Not yesterday, but perhaps the day before? She wasn't sure. She'd been so nervous about what she was planning to do, give herself up to an alpha, she hadn't been able to keep anything down.

Despite the fact she didn't recognize most of the dishes on the table, they all smelled so good and she flitted closer. The table was filled to bursting with more food than she'd ever seen. Tentatively, she reached out for one of the dishes, snagging something that looked like a small pastry. A small nibble later and she groaned, her tastebuds overwhelmed by the sweet treat. She devoured the little cake in a couple of bites and tried another. After her third, she forced herself to slow down. Too much rich food too quickly would make her ill.

Taking a plate, she selected carefully from the table, trying to get a mix of meats and vegetables. A balanced diet wasn't something she'd had the luxury of since before the landing, but she knew it was important. Many of her people had sickened and died of malnutrition since the Tolath arrived.

She was just on her way to sit by the window and look at the parks when the door opened behind her. Turning with a smile, she expected to see Var, but instead a different alien stood in the doorway, his eyes wide with shock.

"You are..." He inhaled deeply, nostrils flaring. "*Omega.*" His voice dropped into a growl that wasn't quite as deep as Var's.

Leia froze, her heart trying to pound its way out of her chest as panic filled her. *Don't run,* came a whisper from the part of her mind still capable of thought. She'd learned that lesson from Var already.

The male stalked toward her, his long legs eating up the distance in a few quick strides. He was huge, but her alpha was bigger.

"Var said he wouldn't share me." The words spilled out of her mouth without thought. "He promised."

His eyes narrowed as he backed her up against the cold window. "I am not Var," he growled. "And you are an omega. Give me your name, little human."

She turned her head as he bent his, her breathing short and panicked as she tried to scoot to the side. A large hand slammed into the window by her shoulder, cutting off her escape.

She didn't dare look at him, but somehow, she managed to find the courage to keep talking. "I belong to A'varen. I am his omega."

"Then he is a fool for leaving you alone. You still have not given me your name, little human." He leaned in close and inhaled again. "An omega. Here. In the citadel..."

She held herself rigid, not wanting him to touch any part of her body. Every cell within her cried out for Var. Having another alpha so close felt wrong. Utterly wrong.

"Var brought me here," she whispered, trying to press herself back into the glass as the alpha breathed in the scent of her skin. "He claimed me. I'm his."

The alpha growled in irritation, the sound making her knees weak. "Name!"

The plate of food fell from her nerveless fingers, missing the soft rug and shattering on the marble floor under her feet.

"My name is Leia, and I belong to Var!" she repeated. Where was he? He said he'd protect her. He promised...

"You are a willful little thing. Pretty, though."

"Get away from her or I will tear your head from

your body and throw it out the window, followed by the rest of you. In pieces," Var growled from the doorway, his voice like thunder.

Leia uttered a strangled cry of relief. "I told him who I belonged to! I told him and he didn't listen!"

"S'jaxx?" Var snarled the strange word at the other man.

The other alpha didn't move, snarling over his shoulder at Var. "She's an *omega*. Here. In the citadel."

Var bellowed and charged, grabbing the other male by the shoulder and hauling him away from Leia. Snarls filled the air, fists flew, and she bolted, desperate to get out of the way and determined to find some way to defend herself. If Var lost to the other man... would that mean she wasn't his anymore? The thought sickened her.

She stumbled against the couch, a cry escaping her as large bodies crashed into and over it. Dodging, she backed up and skittered around the other side of the room, heading for the bedroom. Once inside, her desperate gaze clashed with the wall of weapons. She grabbed the nearest, a deadly looking blade, and backed up around the bed with the weapon held resolutely in front of her. If the alpha killed Var... *oh god*... the blood drained out of her and she took a couple of halting steps toward the door. She had to help him.

Before she could get halfway there, a massive figure filled the doorway, broad shoulders heaving.

"Leia!" Var called her name in harsh tones.

"Are you hurt?" His gaze dropped to the knife in her hands, his expression thunderous. "Why are you armed! Did you think I couldn't protect you?"

He stomped over to her, a hand latching on to her wrist and holding the dagger aside as he crowded into her space, his head bowed over hers. "Are you hurt?"

His grip was hard, and she dropped the dagger like it had burned her. His expression was twisted with fury, his eyes nearly black but not the heated black of before. This cold and dangerous darkness made her tremble.

"No... I'm not. I'm okay," she managed, her voice a bare whisper of sound. The words were broken up as she called to him, the sound halting and broken as she watched him warily. Was he angry with her for the other alpha touching her? "I... I didn't let him. He just... he walked in."

He started to call again, a low, soothing sound that made her want to melt into his arms and hold on tightly.

Chapter 8

"He will never bother you again." He snarled. "And I will be locking that xarthing door from now on."

He took a shuddering breath. "Now, explain why you disobeyed me and took one of my blades, little flower."

"I..." The words died on her lips as she looked up at him. He wasn't angry anymore, at least she didn't think so, but the look in his eyes made her breath catch all over again as a rush of heat dampened the tops of her thighs.

Pressing her legs together she shook her head, wordlessly. She'd disobeyed him. He'd told her not to touch the weapons and she had. Anything she said would get her into more trouble.

"Were you afraid I'd lose?" He sounded insulted. "To S'jaxx? Never. Few in this citadel could take me on and live, and none of them would do so lightly." He breathed in again, and his eyes flashed. "You are bleeding. Where? You told me you weren't hurt!"

"I am?" She looked down, confused. She'd donned one of his shirts, wrapping herself in the soft, warm fabric that carried his scent. It had comforted her and was better than roaming his rooms naked. Her legs were bare, and so were her feet. Her left foot was bleeding a little. She winced, feeling guilty at the stain on the carpet.

"I can clean it up. I must have cut myself when I dropped the plate of food. He... scared me."

Var growled. "I don't care about the xarthing rug. Jaxx caused you to be injured. He will pay for that."

He swung her into his arms. "I'm taking you to the healer now."

9

Bated fury ran through his veins as Var strode out of the bedroom with his injured omega cradled in his arms. Tremors shook her tiny frame, which fed his rage as did the scent of her blood in the air.

Jaxx had managed to get to his feet, nursing a broken nose. He was quick to move out of the way when Var aimed a kick at him.

"She's hurt because of you," he snarled in their language. "Be thankful it's minor or I would gut you and spread your entrails over the main courtyard."

That was still an option. Every part of him that was alpha demanded it. His eyes narrowed dangerously, but the soft, broken parth from the tiny female in his arms brought him back to himself. She was terrified, the sharp stink of her fear cutting through the testosterone in the room like a knife.

Aiming a venomous look at the other alpha, Var set his omega on her feet for a moment. He wrapped the soft blanket from the back of the couch, the one she'd kept touching last night, around her slender form. Taking care, he gathered her up into his arms again before striding for the door.

He paused before he walked out. "Even *look* at my omega again, and I will carve your eyeballs out of your head with a rusty spoon."

"Does the Overseer know you've claimed an omega?" Jaxx's words followed him like a taunt into the corridor.

Var ignored him. He'd deal with that issue later after Leia had seen a healer.

She stayed quiet, though the steady sound of her parth told him she still sought to calm him even as he calmed her. It was strange, the effect she had on him. He could feel the rage fading, and he knew without looking in a mirror that his eyes had changed back to their normal shade. That had never happened so fast.

"Talk to me, little flower. Did you get a chance to eat before he disturbed you? To bathe? Did he touch you?" he demanded sharply. Friend or not, if Jaxx had laid a hand on her...

"No." Her reply was soft. "He just scared me and sniffed me a lot." She shivered. "I didn't like having him so close to me. It felt wrong."

His heart swelled at her words. "Good."

Then he reconsidered. "Not that he scared you. That he didn't touch you."

She shook her head, the slide of her hair over her shoulders tickling the side of his neck. With a small growl, he turned his head and buried his nose in her hair as he walked.

"He didn't," she said quietly, drawing closer to him as they garnered attention again. They were ever likely to, as with Jaxx. Once the other alphas scented an omega, they were fascinated. This time though her fear was more muted. He rumbled his approval. She was more settled and secure in his protection, as she should be.

None of the alphas they passed made the mistake of looking too long or obstructing his path. It was only a matter of minutes before they were outside the doors to the healer's wing—not the one the warriors used, but the one dedicated to seeing to the needs of those who lived within the palace walls.

He walked through the doors with Leia cradled tightly against his chest. "Healer! My omega is injured."

"*Your* omega?" A tall alpha appeared in a side door, an expression of avid curiosity on his face. His gaze flicked to Leia and Var had to bite back a possessive growl. "Bring her in here. I wasn't aware the Lord Overseer had lifted the ban on claiming more omegas. What happened to her?"

Var took a couple of steps into the room but then paused as he reconsidered his plan. Leia was hurt, but the healer was an alpha and therefore a threat. The warning growl started in the back of his throat and he backed up a step at the other male's approach.

"She was injured when I had to beat another alpha for trying to touch her."

"Ah." Healer T'kinn eyed him and then Leia. "I imagine I'll be seeing him shortly, then." He motioned again. "I can't treat her while you're holding her, A'varen."

Var snarled. "Why not?"

T'kinn's lip curled back and he snarled back. "This is my domain. We do this my way, or you can treat her yourself."

Leia put a soft hand on his cheek, that sweet, unsteady parth rising from her throat again. It stole the edge from his anger and brought his focus back to her. His flower. So tiny and delicate... and injured.

"Fascinating." T'kinn stepped forward, head cocked. "She parths?"

Var snarled. "She does. But *not* for you."

The fact that the other alpha could even hear her lovecall annoyed him. She parthed for him and him alone. It was *his*.

"Var," Leia murmured softly. "He's only trying to help."

"*Oi*! Dickhead!" a frustrated female voice called out. "At least put a fucking dressing on her foot. The poor thing is bleeding on your carpet. I still don't understand why you have carpets in here. Everyone who comes in here is a bloody mess."

Var's head snapped up and he looked for the source of the voice. At first, he didn't see anyone, but then he heard a whisper of sound behind him and turned to spot a human female. Her scent almost marked her as an omega, but then he frowned and leaned in a little. No, she wasn't an omega. Something close, but not quite there.

"You. Fix her." He nodded to the new arrival and then at Leia. "I will allow that."

The other female ran a hand through her short blonde hair and then grinned. "I can, sure. But you'll have to ask His Highness, lord of the medical bay, if he'll permit it."

"Lord of the..." Var looked at T'kinn. "Kinn, what is she talking about?"

Kinn shot the female an irritated glance. "She is often difficult and hard to understand."

To his shock, Leia chuckled a little. "I understood her perfectly." She nodded to the other female. "They're really bossy. Aren't they?"

The other woman grinned and approached. "And then some. I'm Serena. You are?"

Var tensed a little as he watched the interplay between the two females. This new one was younger than his Leia, but her open and honest smile to his omega endeared him to her.

"You will help her." He flicked a glance at Kinn. "She will treat Leia."

"This is my..." Kinn snarled in frustration. "Fine. Serena, you will treat this female's injuries. However, I need information, and you will provide it, Var. Starting with where she came from and how long she's been in your possession. Have you claimed her? Knotted her? Is she in heat?"

Leia stirred, her cheeks darkening. "Var? Does he need to know that?"

"Oi! Don't be an asshole. You're embarrassing her," Serena cut in, apparently unconcerned about manners or her own survival. "No, sweetheart, he doesn't need to know that. He just wants to, and these jerks don't seem to understand the difference."

Leia laughed, the light, musical sound capturing his interest yet again, leaving him utterly entranced.

"This is acceptable," he rumbled, following the human woman to one of the treatment bays. Gently, he settled his flower down on the bed and winced as he saw the blood over her delicate foot.

Retreating a couple of steps, he watched as Serena fussed around his omega, her movements practiced and efficient as she started to clean up the cuts on Leia's feet.

Movement out the corner of his eye got his attention and he slammed a hand in the center of Kinn's chest as he attempted to get past him. "*No.*"

Kinn growled at him, his lip curled back, but there was no malice in it. Var dropped his hand and shrugged. "This is not the way I heard it would be. It is but..."

"Explain."

Var kept his eyes on Leia, making sure she didn't show the slightest sign of distress as he talked. "She can parth. And it..." He rubbed the heel of his hand over his breastbone. "It soothes me. And she is difficult." He borrowed Kinn's word. "And stubborn. But she is *mine.*"

"And the rest?"

"Is as it should be. But she is... not." He grunted. "When S'jaxx scared her, she ran and got a dagger. She was coming back to use it." He shook his head, anger and pride filling him. "An omega with a weapon!"

Kinn's eyes widened a little. "That is... definitely unusual. Quite fascinating. My research indicates that human omegas are not the same as in other species."

His gaze settled on Serena as she treated Leia's wounds.

"Some are outspoken and defiant, not meek and biddable as they should be. But the meek ones, the ones that were here when we first arrived, those claimed by the L'crav?" His expression set into stony lines. "They are too meek. I fear they are broken in some way."

Var remembered what Leia had told him about the way the L'crav had acted, the abuse and damage they'd done. "They did this." He told Kinn what he knew and the two men shared a look of horror and rage.

"Such a waste," Kinn said, his voice hard. "Tane must be told about this."

Var tensed. "She is *mine*."

"That remains to be seen. Do you wish to be more forthcoming about things now?"

"No." Var snarled, but he recognized the trap he'd fallen into. "But I will do it to protect her."

Kinn nodded, a sound of approval rumbling from the center of his chest. "Excellent. Have you claimed her? I see your mark. Was knotting successful? Did she start to parth before or after knotting?"

"She is mine. Claimed, knotted and marked." He grinned. "Repeatedly."

He scratched at his jaw. "She parthed after I knotted her the first time."

"Repeatedly? She is in heat?"

Var didn't answer until the healer asked him several more times. "No. Maybe. Her eyes change, she can parth now. But..." He nodded. "She is still stubborn and not entirely in the thrall of a heat. Why is that?"

Kinn flicked his fingers. "That is one of the things our lord has tasked me with finding out."

Var grunted in frustration, and the healer continued, a thoughtful look on his face. Arms folded over his chest, Kinn stroked his chin with long fingers.

"She is older than most omegas I have seen," he mused. "She is underweight and looks tired. Even with the drives and instincts of an omega to mate, the body is protective. If she does not have the resources to carry a child to term, her body will not allow conception or allow her to enter heat because it would be dangerous to her."

"She couldn't carry a child to term right now? It would harm her?" The news hit Var hard. "How much food does she need for that to happen? To be safe? How much rest?"

Kinn shot him a look that was dangerously close to amusement. "You'll know when the time comes."

"She has a daughter. Another omega. Do you think these omegas will all breed true?"

Kinn hummed thoughtfully. "We can hope. There's so much about these humans we do not understand."

"Are you two done nattering over there? If so, she's good to go," Serena announced. "But you're welcome to come back here any time you like to get those cuts checked. Isn't she, Your Highness?"

Kinn's expression set into unamused lines. "My name is T'kinn of the H'thor, not 'Your Highness.' I am not royal."

Var hid his smile at the healer's comment. Seemed he'd managed to find a human female as headstrong as he was. Moving to Leia's side, he offered her a gentle smile. Relieved that she was healed, he scooped her up. The need to get her out of here and back to his bed, where he could reassure himself she was unharmed, overwhelmed all else.

He paused for a moment, Leia in his arms, to look at the other human female. "She needs to be checked? Will she not heal properly?"

"I'll heal just fine." Leia leaned her head on his shoulder. "But I might like to visit anyway. Unless you plan on locking me in your rooms?"

"I might," he grumbled, but then he looked at Serena and realized what his omega was really asking for. "But if you wish to visit, you may." He turned to look at T'kinn.

"And Healer T'kinn will not harass you with questions or try to touch you while you are here. Correct?"

Serena eyed him for a moment and then smirked. "I think I might like you. Definitely more than him."

Var hefted Leia gently closer to his chest. "I have my omega. I do not need another."

"Oh, now I know I'm going to like you," Serena said approvingly and then shot a sidelong look at Kinn as she slipped out of the room before adding... "Take notes, dickhead."

"Ignore her waffle," Kinn grumbled. "I think she might be mentally defective."

Leia snorted, and Var looked down to see her eyes sparkling with amusement. "What is it, little flower?" he asked, giving her permission to speak in front of the other alpha.

"I think she's nice, and more than capable. Definitely not mentally defective," she shot a look at Kinn. "Unfortunately, some men, when faced with a strong woman, instantly dismiss her as broken in some way."

Kinn's brows raised almost to his hairline. "See to your omega, Var. And when you come back here, Leia, remember this is my hall and I will expect your respect. Or I will take it up with your alpha."

"She will be respectful, or I will punish her," Var stated before turning and walking away quickly so Kinn didn't see the smile he was fighting to hide.

"That was dangerous, little flower," he murmured as they left.

"No, it wasn't." She gave him that same innocent look as before. "You promised to protect me."

He uttered a strangled laugh "Yes, I did. But I didn't expect you to test that theory so soon."

10

Leia cuddled up into Var's arms as he carried her back to their rooms. *Their* rooms. When had she started to think of them that way?

A small sigh escaped her as she settled her head against his shoulder. Closing her eyes, she allowed herself to relax. She was tired from last night and the tension today... she didn't bounce back easily these days, if she ever had. Living in fear for years would wear anyone out.

"I brought you clothes and some other things I thought you might like," he said as they approached the door to their rooms.

"You brought me clothes?"

She'd traded almost everything she had for the

dress she'd worn yesterday. She had nothing left to her name now. Not even shoes.

"I did. And a comb for your hair. And creams for your skin. There are boots, too. Fur lined. To keep your feet warm. You can see it all soon."

He walked into their room, but instead of setting her on her feet, he kept going, straight to his bedroom. "Right after I punish you."

"What?" She stiffened and tried to push her way out of his grip, but it was like trying to wrestle with a tree or a statue. He didn't even seem to notice she was trying.

"Did you think I would forget what you did?" He spun around to nod toward the wall of weapons. "I told you not to touch anything on that wall."

"I was coming to help you!" She gasped as he dropped her on the bed. She tried to skitter away, making it to the top of the bed and pulling her feet out of his reach.

"Did I, or did I not tell you not to touch anything on that wall?" he grumbled.

"Well yes. But you were in trouble!"

He snorted. "From Jaxx? Not on his best day." He stripped off his shirt without taking his eyes from her. Removing his gunbelt, he set it aside. Only then did he undo his pants, sliding them over his muscular legs as his cock bobbed up to strike his carved stomach.

"You disobeyed."

"I was helping," she protested, not moving an inch despite the sudden heat that flooded through her. Her clit pulsed in time to her pounding heart, and part of her wanted to reach for him and draw him into bed with her.

He crooked a finger at her and then pointed to the edge of the bed. "Hands and knees. There. Now."

She didn't move for a second, his eyes getting darker and darker with each second that passed.

"Fight me all you like, little flower. I will just enjoy this more."

Heat rather than fear rolled through her as the tension in the room ramped up. Flicking a glance to the door, she made a slight movement toward the side of the bed.

He barked a short laugh. "Oh, run... *Please* run, little flower. Remember what I told you? We're predators."

Something inside her snapped. "You mean you're assholes!" The taunt was out of her mouth before she could reconsider.

The effect on Var was instantaneous. He lunged

for her, catching hold of her ankles and pulling her to the edge of the bed. His hand was still wrapped around one ankle, his black eyes gleaming and teeth bared against the dark scruff of his beard. "Want to try that again?"

"Asshole alpha. I was helping!"

She knew she was pouring gasoline on an open fire, but part of her was relishing the moment. She could make this towering monster of an alpha snap. Whatever this punishment would be, she had a sneaking suspicion she'd like it more than she wanted to admit.

"One last chance." His voice was velvet temptation over steel. "Hands and knees. *Now.*"

"Screw you!" she spat back, glaring up at him as she made a show of trying to get away. Not seriously, though. Not just because there was no point and he'd catch her in a heartbeat. It was more because she liked the way his eyes darkened as she forced him to hold on to her, the muscles flexing and tensing in his chest and shoulders as she kicked out to shake his grip on her ankle.

"Not how this is going to go." His voice was the distant thunder of an oncoming storm. Even as he held her, his thumb traced small circles across her skin, leaving shimmering heat in the wake of his touch.

He moved without warning and lifted her.

"Hey!" she yelped, kicking out at him with her injured foot.

He managed to dodge her kick, grunting in annoyance. "You're going to reopen the cuts. Don't be foolish."

His words made her slow, and he took advantage of her lapse to manhandle her into the position she'd been trying to avoid—on her hands and knees at the edge of the bed.

He stood off to one side, one big hand fisting in the over-large shirt she'd borrowed and using it like a handle to control her. Her cheeks burned as he yanked it up, exposing her nakedness to his avid gaze. Then he spanked her, delivering a stinging slap to punctuate each growled word. "Never. Touch. My. Weapons."

She squealed and called him names, bucking and trying to escape the stinging heat of his palm against her ass. He was spanking her but wasn't hurting her. Sure, each strike of his hand stung a little, but then he rubbed over her burning skin with a featherlight touch that left tingles in its wake. It was all she could do not to arch her back and push back against him.

Every blow landed in a different spot, and soon her ass felt warm and sensitive. He paused in his punishment, and she tensed, not sure what to expect. When his mouth grazed the heated flesh of one cheek, she couldn't hold back the moan that rose from her throat. His breath fanned over her skin as she heard the now-familiar sound of him breathing in her scent.

"Who do you belong to?" he asked, his voice still hard. She could hear the need in it, though, the weight of his desire enriching every word.

The need to fight abandoned her, and she arched her back, her voice a soft whisper of submission. "You. I belong to you, A'varen of the H'thor."

Head hung, she waited for his reply, her entire body taut with heat and need. His breathing was harsh, tension stretching out between them until she could scream with it.

"Yes, you do."

He moved in behind her, his hard body pressed against her hot skin. She sucked in a breath, expecting him to take her immediately, but he reached between her thighs and drew his fingers through her slick folds.

"So wet. I think you enjoyed your punishment, little flower." He stroked her clit. "Did you like it?"

"No," she replied stubbornly, trying to hold still as his touch caused tingles through her blood. Her hands bunched in the bedding and she parted her thighs a little in a silent request for more.

"Liar."

He circled her clit. She rocked her hips, trying to make him touch her where she needed it the most, and his hand landed on her ass again, a barely there slap that was more warning than punishment.

"Your pleasure is mine, little flower. I will grant it to you when I am ready."

"Asshole," she muttered.

He was an alpha, and the import of that took her breath away. He was an alpha and he hadn't hurt her. He'd claimed her and knotted her but it hadn't been as the stories and rumors said it would be. It had been... good. Better than good. She'd never much been into sex, even before the Tolath conquered. She'd caught with Savannah during a brief relationship that had quickly fizzled out.

Now? She shivered with anticipation of Var's touch. Needed him to touch her. Ached for him to fill her again.

He chuckled. "Now that is an interesting suggestion." He slid a finger along the crease between her cheeks. "One day. When you are ready. But not today."

"I didn't mean that!" she squeaked, the sound devolving into a frustrated moan as he withheld the touch she needed.

He flicked his finger across her clit again, so quickly it was over before she could truly enjoy it.

"You are beautiful, little flower. Always. But now, like this..." He breathed in hard. "You are breathtaking."

Heat escaped her again, a white-hot trickle down her thigh that made her press her flaming cheeks to the cool sheets. He knew what he was doing to her, and he was enjoying it. He was a monster, an utter monster.

He growled as the proof of her need spilled out of her, coating his fingers. "We'll discuss what you meant another time."

He finally gave her what she needed, working her swollen clit with a deft touch that sent her senses spiraling. "We are done talking. Come for me, Leia. *Now.*"

If any other male had tried that, she'd have laughed at him. But this was Var. And when he ordered her to come, her body responded. It was maddening and wonderful. She rode his fingers, her inner walls pulsing as every part of her reached for release. She imagined him inside her, the feel of him, hard and huge, filling her impossibly full.

"Var!" she called his name as she came. Her breathing was hard pants as her back arched to shove her hips back against him.

"Oh god," she murmured brokenly, her face against the sheets as she quivered and squirmed for him. He was still a monster, but... god did he know how to touch her.

He leaned over her, dusting gentle kisses to her back and shoulders. *"My flower."* Then he positioned himself at her entrance, one arm wrapping around her waist to lift her up as he eased himself into her body. "Mine."

She was still quivering when he took her, and it was almost enough to trigger another orgasm. She moaned and gripped the sheets as he claimed her, but somehow she managed to laugh too. "I think we've established that."

He snarled and thrust the last few inches. "Mine!" he repeated, the word almost lost in a guttural growl.

She gasped as he filled her, hard and fast. Each

ridge parted her a little more until he was buried balls deep. Whimpering, she wrapped her hand around his wrist. His lips found her shoulder, the hard, biting kiss warning her he was close to the edge of his control.

But, rather than that thought sparking fear, she relaxed, melting against him. "Yours," she turned her head to whisper, offering her lips for his kiss.

He claimed her mouth hungrily as he powered into her, but there was a tenderness to his touch. His parth rumbled between them, ramping up her desire until she was nothing but flames and need. Another orgasm bloomed, longer and slower than the one before. Every thrust of his hips stretched it out a little longer until she was lost in the pleasure of it all.

She felt his knot swell even before he came, his last few strokes unsteady. The rhythm broken, his cock thickened and then they locked into place as he roared in release. His entire body went rigid as he emptied himself inside her. Thanks to his knot she felt every pulse of his cock and heated jet of his seed within her as he came.

She trembled in his arms, not missing the care in his touch as he held them both upright. Their breathing was harsh in the sudden silence, and she turned her head to kiss the thick swell of his shoulder where he propped them up. Contentment washed through her, a feeling she never thought she'd experience with an alpha before she came here. But now she realized it wasn't just any alpha... it was Var.

"*My alpha,*" she murmured softly, body soft and pliant with sensual exhaustion.

11

She had accepted him. Fully. Wonder and contentment filled Var, two emotions he'd rarely experienced in his life. His little flower had surrendered to him, and it had been glorious.

He still didn't understand why she wasn't like the others. Her mind was as sharp as her tongue and wits. But he didn't care about the why anymore. She was perfect. Maddening, willful, and *his*.

He held her close, enjoying the peace of the moment. It was the same feeling he'd been seeking when he'd driven out into the barrens yesterday. Now, he had it with him, always. He smiled and nuzzled her neck, knowing his next word would make his little flower smile. "Mine."

Her soft laugh was music to his ears. "You like that word."

He grinned and nipped her neck lightly, right over his mark, and savored the way she clenched around him. "You *are* mine. Do you deny it?"

She shook her head, shivering as he kissed under her ear. She was so soft, her silken skin a siren's call under his callused hands. But then the healer's words came back to him. His flower was tired and underfed, both conditions he needed to rectify before she would enter heat for him. He couldn't wait until her belly was swollen with his child. More than that, he wanted to see her well-fed and laughing, the shadows banished from beneath her eyes.

Once his knot released, he eased out of her and rose from the bed. "Stay."

He went to the bathing chamber, found the softest cloth he had, and soaked it in warm water. Then, he returned and cleaned her, tending to her body and making her comfortable.

"You don't need to do that." She tried to evade his hands at first, but a warning growl made her lie still.

"I do. This is the way of things. It is my honor and duty to take care of you." He paused in his ministrations to meet her gaze. "Always. Do you understand now?"

She watched him, an odd expression on her beautiful face as she lay there and let him tend to her. There was no fear in her scent now and no tension in her body when she looked at him, though he could see her sharp mind working behind her forest-green eyes. Like she was making a decision about something although he had no idea what it was, and he suspected he would not be able to compel her to tell him.

She was very different from the omegas of other species. Those were all docile and meek-mannered. But his omega had fire and spark, and with that came more rewards than simply a soft pussy to fuck and a womb to breed his children. He liked it when she spoke, and he *wanted* to talk to her. Learn more about her and her view of the world.

Setting the cloth aside, he sat down beside her and opened his arms to her. "You will eat now."

She sat up and curled into his arms with a musical laugh that filled his soul. "Why yes, thank you. I think I will."

"Good." He gathered her up and carried her into the other room, grabbing another blanket from the back of a chair as he passed. He sat down at the end of the table and handed her the blanket.

As she draped it over her legs, he started to fill a plate for her. He realized he had no idea what she might like, so he took one of everything he could reach. It bothered him that almost none of it had been touched. T'kinn was right. She needed feeding.

When the plate was stacked as high as he could manage, he set it down in front of them and chose a morsel at random. "This is klavva. One of my favorites," he told her and held it to her lips. "Eat."

"What is it?" she asked, but rather than wait for his answer, she parted her lip and took the morsel, trusting him. A warm feeling spread through his chest.

"Oh..." She moaned, an expression of bliss on her face as she chewed. "That is amazing."

He offered her another bite. "It is a..." He had to search his mind to come up with the correct word in her language. "Pastry. My mother used to make them for me when I was a boy."

"Your mother." Leia shook her head. "It never occurred to me that you'd have one."

He arched a brow. "Did you think we sprang from the ground fully formed? Of course I had a mother."

She took another bite, finishing off the treat he held out for her, and then answered when she was done. "Was she... like me? An omega?"

A flush of pleasure filled him at her question. She wanted to learn about him and his kind. This boded well.

"She was an omega, yes. Like you?" He shook his head. "No."

He gave himself time to organize his thoughts by selecting another item from the plate and offering it to her. "This is something you might recognize. Cow. But prepared with our spices it is quite tasty."

He waited until she took a bite of the offered meat before speaking. "You humans are not like other omegas. We have claimed many worlds and created many omegas. None are like you. Stubborn." He kissed her temple. "But smart."

She hummed with pleasure as she took a bite. He liked watching her, already imagining the gauntness gone from her frame and cheeks, her skin flushed with health.

"Other omegas are not stubborn? Or not smart?" she asked, watching him as he selected another morsel for her. Her lips parted in anticipation this time and her teeth grazed his fingertips in her eagerness for the tidbit.

"They are not either of those things. They are biddable. Obedient." He took a moment to select her next tidbit—a bit of fruit he thought she might like. "And other omegas welcome the attention of any alpha. They crave our touch and our protection."

Leia snorted. "Definitely not the same then."

She bit into the fruit, but this time, he didn't let go. She had to suck at his fingers to free the morsel, and the sensation went straight to his cock. She gave him a broad smile as she managed to get the fruit and then licked a drop of juice off his fingertips, looking him right in the eye as she did so.

He growled at her. "*Behave.* You need food and rest before you can have my cock again."

"Bossy," she informed him and then pointed to the plate. "Some of the pink stuff next?"

She was giving him orders, but he didn't mind. The fact that she sat happily in his lap and ate, no scent of fear at all on her skin, made him happy. She could give him all the orders she liked as long as she kept eating. Because the more she ate, the quicker she would be healthy and then she would go into heat. When she did... he wouldn't stop taking her until she was carrying his child.

He rubbed the side of his neck absently. Once she was in heat, she might mark him, too. He wanted that. He wanted every male in the citadel to know he had an omega. It was a badge of honor, but so far, no human omega had marked their alpha that way. It was thought that they didn't have that drive.

He handed her a glass full of salla berry juice. "Drink."

She wrinkled her nose at the contents. "It's blue."

"It's good for you. Drink."

Her little glare over the top of the glass made him smile. She was willful but she did as she was told, mostly. After one sip, she curled her lip. "I don't like that. It tastes funny."

He took the glass from her and set it back on the table. "Then you don't have to drink it." He offered her more of the klavva he'd given her first. He liked watching her eat things that pleased her.

She ate it happily, making tiny noises of pleasure that turned his cock to stone. He knew she could feel it, because she drew out every moan and sigh, squirming in his lap until he had to grit his teeth to stop from taking her right there on the table.

Slowly, though, her antics quieted and she lapsed into periods of contented silence between bites of food. Sensing her exhaustion, he began a soft call, the low rumble soothing her. When her head hit his chest and her breathing deepened, he held her and let her sleep.

His omega.

When she woke, they would talk more. He'd learn what he could about her offspring, and then he'd fulfill his promise to her.

He'd find her daughter.

Well-fed and warm, his little omega had slept the clock around and was still asleep when Var left his quarters, prompted into action by a summons from his lord. The guards on Lord Tane's quarters nodded to him as he passed, not daring to challenge him. If any of them did, they wouldn't survive more than a few minutes.

"I understand, my lord. But I would perhaps suggest that you allow the quarter celebration to go ahead. Times have been hard for the beta population recently, what with the recent change of power... this will allow them something to look forward to."

The calming voice of the human mother superior reached his ears before he entered the lord's inner sanctum, so it was no surprise to see the tiny, delicate beta standing in the middle of the polished floor.

Chapter 11

Var took a deep breath. Only three scents were in the room. His, Lord Tane's, and the dull, muted scent of the Mother Superior, barely any emotion in the light floral scent he always associated with her.

When he'd first arrived, he'd thought the beta priestess was the most beautiful thing he'd ever seen and counted himself fortunate to look upon her. He'd even harbored a small fantasy that she would one day be realized as an omega and he could fight for the right to claim her. But the instant he'd seen Leia in her red dress, any thoughts of other females had been blown to atoms.

Lord Tane stood by the window, his hands clasped behind his back as he looked out over the city.

Var claimed a spot beside the door and waited, hands at his side, eyes ahead. His Lord would speak to him when he was ready.

"I understand your request, Mother Superior, but now is not the time for celebrations." Tane pointed out the window. "First, there must be order. And I do not see order out there." He dropped his hand. "Your people resist. Why would I reward them for that?"

Var was tempted to speak, but he held his tongue. The question hadn't been for him. He needed to tell his lord some things, though. Soon. He was beginning to understand why the humans resisted them.

Mother Superior's expression didn't alter. It was as calm as always, her hands folded elegantly before her. "My people resist because they do not see the difference between the L'crav and the H'thor. Perhaps the quarter celebrations would allow them to see that you and your males are different?"

It was a softly worded statement but one with a lot of power. Var could see why Tane allowed her audience. She had a way of getting to the heart of a matter and verbalizing it—an unusual quality in a beta.

Tane remained silent for another few seconds, a rare sign that he was reconsidering. When he turned, his jaw was tight.

"We are nothing alike. Why is this not obvious to them?" He waved off any reply. "Don't bother explaining. I know why."

She cocked her head to one side, one hand resting on the circular pendant at her breast. "They are afraid."

Var blinked. The tiny female had just defied the Lord Overseer. It was a small act, but still...

Chapter 11

Tane chose to ignore it. "A half-day, then. No more."

"Thank you, my lord." She inclined her head, keeping her gaze down as she waited to be dismissed. Lord Tane studied her for long moments, time enough for the slightest edge of confusion and wariness to edge into the Mother Superior's scent.

"Dismissed," he said, waving his hand although Var noted his gaze didn't leave her as she walked from the room. Then he turned his attention to Var.

Of all of them, Lord Tane was the closest to the Tolath ideal. Not only highblood, he was one of the younger princes of the Thoracian bloodline, the reason he had been granted an overseer position so young. That stroke of luck had afforded them all the opportunity of a new, albeit failing planet, and the possibility of finding omegas of their own.

Var bowed his head. "My lord, you wished to speak to me?"

"I did." Tane didn't move, but everything about him became more focused, as if poised on the edge of violence. "You requested personal time. I granted it. Now, I have heard you have an omega in your rooms. Explain how that is when I have decreed no omegas are to be claimed."

"Her name is Leia. She offered herself in trade.

She is..." Var tapped a fist to his heart. "She is mine, Lord. Her scent. It was perfect." He raised his head for a moment, letting Tane see the truth in his eyes before dropping his gaze again. "She parths for me. My lord. She is *mine*."

Tane's growl of anger was cut off in surprise. "She does? Humans don't do that. Oh for Kranov's sake, stop looking at the floor like some xarthing beta," he snapped. "She parths for you. Are you sure?"

Var looked up and nodded. An omega's lovecall was a beautiful thing, but it could not be coerced. An omega chose to bestow it or not. An unhappy omega did not parth for their alpha.

"I am sure. Jaxx can confirm it. He heard her."

"Explain how you knew she was the one."

Var described her scent, and the surety that came the moment he breathed it in. "Her eyes change, too. Kinn said once she is in better health, she will go into heat." He couldn't keep the pride out of his voice. "She will bear my children. And in exchange, I have promised to find her adult daughter. Another omega."

Tane's brow quirked. "She has an omega daughter?"

"She does. The female was taken not long ago."

Tane snarled. "Against my orders?"

Var inclined his head.

"I believe so, yes lord. Leia..." he frowned. "Things are not as we... I expected. I believed that human omegas were simply so rare we had not found many. But..."

He met Tane's gaze directly.

"I now do not think this is the case. Leia told me..." He stopped and took a breath to quell the rage that still rolled through him. "Not long after they arrived, the L'crav went on a rampage. They hunted down and raped the omegas. Often repeatedly. Leia says many did not survive. The others, it appears, went into hiding."

"They *what?*" Tane roared, a sound of raw fury that shook the walls of the citadel.

Var waited until his lord was quiet, though he knew better than to think the male was calm.

"Leia was terrified. Even as she made her offer, I could smell the fear on her. She is smarter than the others, my lord. Intelligent, even. And stubborn. Even now." He smiled a little. "In fact, more so now she understands matters better. She thought I would hurt her. That the knotting would be painful."

He scrubbed a hand through his hair. "She believed she would endure nothing but suffering and abuse at my hands. This is what they think we are, my lord."

"What?"

Var could count the number of times he'd seen his lord surprised on the fingers of one hand, even if he chopped a couple off. Right now, Tane was stunned and made no effort to hide it.

"They think we would *harm* an omega? Abuse one? What in Kranov's name do they think we are?" Tane closed his eyes and rubbed a hand over his short beard. "So... the omegas *are* here, but in hiding? How? How have they hidden from us for so long?"

"I don't know, my lord. Perhaps they're all like my Leia? There's one with Kinn, but I'm not sure she *is* an omega. Her scent is... wrong."

Tane's eyes darkened. "*T'kinn* has an omega?"

Var cursed inwardly. What had the xarthing healer been doing keeping secrets from their lord? "I'm not sure she is. And he has not claimed her. I think he is learning more about them."

"Indeed." There was a wealth of meaning in that word. "Where did you find this omega of yours?"

Var explained quickly, knowing Tane needed every detail. "At Clearwater. Though I don't believe that is where she's been hiding. I believe she traveled some distance. She is tired, my lord. And underfed.

She had nothing with her but the clothes on her back."

Tane nodded, his expression not giving away any indication of his mood. It didn't need to. His eyes were black enough.

"You have seen to her comfort?" he asked, studying Var. He knew what his lord was looking for and turned his head side to side so Tane could see his unmarked neck.

"She has not marked me yet. Kinn said she could not carry a child to term at the moment so her body will not allow her to go into heat." He knew that would be something Tane would be particularly interested in. Tane's father was cruel and known to breed his omegas to the point of death, discarding them when they became too weak. Tane's mother had been one of them.

"Do you think she will mark you when she's ready?" Tane asked, his tone thoughtful. "I haven't heard of that happening yet. Not with these humans."

"I believe so. They are different but still omegas." He shrugged. "Kinn could likely tell you more. But what the Mother Superior said about them fearing us? They have reason, my lord. Leia has no understanding of the differences between the L'crav and the H'thor. They think us all the same." He snarled. "The xarthing L'crav were fools."

Tane focused on him. "But she has a daughter? And Kinn has some kind of omega also? So that is three?"

He folded his arms over his chest. Though he was leaner than Var, he wouldn't dare to take the lord on in a fight. "I will speak to all of them."

At Var's unexpected growl, a hint of a smile curved his lips. "Have no fear. I would not claim my shield's omega."

Var managed to keep his hands from fisting and silenced the snarl that threatened to rise from his throat. Challenging Tane was suicide. His response had been automatic, not meant as a challenge.

"Thank you." He ground the words out between gritted teeth. "I should warn you. These females are not..." He shook his head. "They can be defiant. Difficult. And I have not yet located my omega's daughter. I was focused on Leia's needs until now."

"They are omega—"

Tane's words were cut off by the sound of a female scream from somewhere else in the citadel. Var's blood ran cold as the sound registered.

"*Leia.*"

12

Leia had woken up feeling better than she had in years. Maybe decades. She'd bathed and dressed in the new clothes Var had brought for her, pulling on the fur-lined boots with coos of delight. She wiggled her toes as she walked, liking the way the fur felt against her skin.

Fresh food had been set out for her, and she grazed through the offerings, but for the first time in her life, she wasn't terribly hungry. It was a strange feeling. So was being left alone. The rooms didn't feel right without Var there. He'd left no note, but she couldn't read the chicken scratch the Tolath used and she had no idea if their language uploads included written words. There was so much about them that no one knew. She smiled. Including the fact that not all of them were violent bullies.

Feeling guilty about not eating all the food, she wrapped up a selection of the pastries in a napkin and ventured to the door. It opened to reveal a human servant on the other side.

"I'd like to visit the medical center, please," she said, holding her little haul carefully. "Which way is it?"

She expected to be told that Var had forbidden her to leave their rooms but the beta merely bowed. "This way."

She stayed close to the servant, making sure her hair was swept off her neck so Var's mark was clearly visible. She knew who she belonged to, and she was starting to understand that it wasn't just about ownership. It was about protection. Hers.

Several men eyed her as she walked past them, but none of them did more than stare and breathe in deeply, nostrils flaring. They kept their distance and she relaxed a little. These alphas weren't so bad, after all.

"*Omega.*"

The growl took her by surprise. Low and dangerous, it sounded all kinds of wrong as a huge alpha stepped in front of her. Tall and broad-shouldered, he was easily as big as Var, but his features were cruel and hard.

"I belong to A'varen of the H'thor," she said clearly, backpedaling a few steps to get away. Her back hit something solid and warm. She whirled around to look up into another alpha's face. His expression was hard, the same as the first one.

She felt a spike of fear, her instincts screaming to run and hide, to find a small space and stay there until Var found her. She knew better. Running would only make it worse.

Standing her ground, she held her head high and tried to project an air of confidence. "I belong to A'varen of the H'thor, the Shield of Lord Overseer Tane. Let me pass."

"The shield is not here," the first one spoke. His words were accented, the sound harsher.

"If he wanted to keep you, he should have tied you to his bed." A hard hand clamped down on her shoulder, fingers tightening to the point of pain. "Where an omega belongs."

She suppressed a gasp, her mind racing a mile a minute. She had no chance against even one alpha, never mind two. If she was sensible, she wouldn't fight, but everything within her rebelled at the idea.

The touch of the one who held her made her feel sick and the idea of more...

Turning her head, she bit the alpha's hand, throwing her pastries into the face of the other one. The one she bit roared, letting her go, and she ran.

And screamed...

From somewhere up ahead, she heard an alpha roar. *Var*. She sprinted toward the sound, praying she could keep out of the alphas' reach long enough for Var to find her. He was her protector, the safe place she needed to reach.

She heard a crash, and then the sound of thundering footsteps got louder every second.

He was coming.

She ran harder, terror giving her feet wings. She wasn't fast enough. Someone grabbed her wrist, hauling her backward with enough force she bit back a scream of pain as her shoulder was wrenched and twisted behind her.

She fought through the pain, lashing out blindly. Her nails tore into flesh, her feet pounding against her captor's legs as he dragged her into his arms.

"Var!" she screamed her alpha's name.

He bellowed hers in return.

He charged into view, bouncing off the far wall as he entered the corridor, his eyes black, fangs bared, clawed hands raised as he came to her rescue. He was the same violent monster she'd seen take down B'rex, but she wasn't afraid of him anymore.

"Hold her!" the alpha who had her bellowed, shoving her toward a smaller male.

A small pack of them had two blank-eyed omegas huddled against the wall. Instinctively, she knew those women were shared between them all. The thought brought a hot rush of bile and she screamed again, kicking her new captor. He snarled and turned her around, just as battle was joined in the center of the corridor.

"He will lose and you will be ours," he snarled in her ear.

"The hell he will," she spat back. She slashed her nails across the alpha's arms. She might as well have been trying to claw steel, but now she'd started fighting, she saw no reason to stop.

Var fought like a demon, a blur of fists and raw fury she could barely track. She barely recognized him as the same male who had wrapped her in a blanket and hand fed her tidbits the day before. That had been Var, her alpha. This was A'varen, the Shield.

He hammered her attacker with blow after blow, grunts of pain almost drowning out the sickening sound of bones and flesh giving way. She winced but forced herself to watch. Var was going to win. Her lip quivered. He had to.

She whimpered as the other alpha knocked him to the ground and for one awful moment, she thought that was it. He was down. If he lost... she... *oh god.*

But instead of sprawling across the floor of the corridor unconscious, Var bounced off the floor, spinning and throwing a hard leg to sweep the other alpha's legs from under him.

She screamed, urging him on. The alpha holding her slapped a hand across her mouth and dragged her backward. Away from Var.

No.

She sank her teeth into his finger and lashed out with her feet again. This time, she got the angle right and managed to drive her heel into his balls. The male groaned, his grip slipping, and she spat out his hand to tear herself free. Dropping to the floor, she crawled back through the crowd, dodging reaching hands until she could see Var again.

He had one knee pressed into the alpha's chest, pummeling him over and over with bloody fists, his face a mask of rage.

She scrambled forward, half stumbling, half

crawling toward him until she was kneeling a few feet away. Var's eyes were completely black, his face a mask of rage. She reached out for him but stopped. Instinct warned her not to get between them so she did the only thing she could think of.

She called to him, her parth low and soft.

13

Death was all around him. He could smell it. Taste it. The alpha who had dared to take his omega was dead, but he beat at the corpse. A message had to be sent. A warning.

Then another scent touched his senses—a whisper of something pure and perfect. Leia.

He took a breath and then another, the rage subsiding as he heard her calling him back from the darkness. His hands fell to his sides, fists unclenching. The ruined face of the male he'd beaten was forgotten as he rose to his feet.

"Leia." He reached out a blood-soaked hand. Then he heard a mewling cry as one of the other omegas threw herself at him, wrapping thin arms around his thigh as her face nuzzled at his crotch.

Leia's eyes turned black in an instant, her soft rumbling fading to a snarl. "Mine."

He caught his breath, the female wrapped around his leg forgotten for a moment as he took in the glory of his omega in all her fury. Her black-on-black gaze focused on the other omega and she snarled viciously in challenge.

The other female cried in fear and pressed closer to Var. He moved to prise her off, but when he reached for her, Leia's snarl got deeper and more vicious.

"My lord..." he started, not taking his eyes off of Leia.

Tane moved away from the wall. Var knew he'd seen everything and would have questions, but right now his only concern was for his omega.

"Someone find the Mother Superior," Tane snapped. He pried the unwanted omega's hand away from Var's thigh. She whimpered in protest but didn't fight. Instead, she turned to Tane, throwing her arms around his waist and clinging like a limpet, making small noises of fear and appeasement.

"Thank you, lord."

Leia was at his side in a heartbeat, plastering herself to him, her hands locked into his shirt and her leg twined around his. She burrowed her face into his chest, her lovecall loud enough for everyone to hear. He parthed back, the instinctive need to comfort her overriding all else.

Tane nodded, looking down at the omega clinging to him with a shuttered expression. "See to *your* omega, my shield."

The words hung in the air. His omega. Those words, spoken by the Lord Overseer himself, changed everything.

"Yes, my lord." He gathered Leia into his arms and cradled her against his chest. "You are not hurt?"

"No." She was rubbing at her lips, her mouth drawn down in an expression of distaste. That's when he saw the blood. Another alpha's blood.

"You bit one of them!" he snarled.

"Two."

"Never again." He raised her higher, so she was looking into his eyes. "You bite no one but me!"

"I was helping!" she hissed at him, a flare of anger in her eyes. She struggled to be free and plastered herself against him, her parth tinged with fury. Her movements against him brought his cock to full attention, but then he realized what she was doing... Replacing the other omega's scent with her own.

He looked down at her, his lovecall deepening at

this new, possessive behavior from his omega. Then she surged up his body, wrapping her arms around his neck. Glaring at the omega in Tane's hold, she nipped Var's neck pointedly.

Lust slammed through him, pushing every other thought aside. He growled and stalked off, leaving Tane and the others to deal with the fallout.

"You're dismissed," Tane called after him, the vaguest hint of amusement in his tone. "I'll expect a proper introduction to your omega soon."

"Thank you, my lord."

Leia pressed herself against him, her mouth on his neck. Every time she nipped him, his cock jerked and throbbed. He was tempted to push her up against the nearest flat surface and take her, but he wouldn't. No one saw his omega naked but him. Her body and her pleasure were his and his alone.

The walk back was utter torture and absolute heaven all at the same time. He'd dreamed of Leia responding to him like this, of her bite on his neck, and now it was here, he reveled in it.

He crashed through the door to their quarters, hooking it with the heel of his boot to slam it shut. Then he turned and pinned her up against the wall, her slender form between his hard body and it.

Chapter 13

Pulling back, he looked down at her and growled. Her eyes were totally black.

"*Yes...*"

"Var," she panted his name, her voice thick with need.

"You are unhurt?" He needed to hear her say it again.

She nodded. "You came before they could do anything. You protected me."

Her words inflamed him to the point of madness. "I will always protect you." He tore at her clothes, needing the feel of her naked body against his skin. She did the same, the two of them making short work of their outfits despite the fact he wouldn't let her go. *Couldn't* let her go. Not ever.

Her small hands found his cock and freed it, her fingertips teasing and light, her breathing coming in hard, fast little pants that made him harder. Some part of his brain whispered that she wasn't ready for him yet, that he had to slow down, to prepare her. But then she levered herself upward, wriggling until he was seated at her entrance, and settled herself around him, taking him into the welcoming heat of her body with a cry that made his cock throb.

"*Xarth!*" he hissed, every cell in his body on fire.

She was so tight around him that he nearly came

there and then. The expression of pleasure on her beautiful face was wondrous, the stuff dreams were made of, but nothing would ever get to him as much as her heat-darkened eyes.

"Careful," he murmured when she made to move again, trying to hold her still so he didn't hurt her. She was slick and wet, but she was still tiny and he was slightly larger in this form. Instead of heeding him, though, she snarled in anger, like a little kitten in a rage.

"*Leia...*" he growled her name, partly in warning, partly in wonder.

She raked her claws across his neck, bucking her hips against him and driving him deeper into her heat.

"Mine," she whispered.

"Yes." *Xarth*, yes. He was hers.

Her eyes gleamed with a wild, feral light. She moved again, and this time he moved with her, too far gone to fight against what they both needed. He tried to move slowly, but she refused to do the same.

Bucking and moaning as she took what she needed, he let her take for a while, savoring her need for him. He revelled in the fact she *was* challenging him for dominance. It was like nothing he'd ever heard of before, but it was amazing at the same time.

Chapter 13

He wasn't passive for long. He couldn't be. He was an alpha and those instincts surged to the fore. She mewled in need and welcome as he took over, thrusting harder and deeper.

She clung to him, her nails biting into his skin. Burying her face in the crook of his shoulder, she shuddered as her inner walls tightened around him, heralding her imminent release.

His cock swelled as she flexed around its length, the feel of her mouth on his neck enough to push him to the edge of his control. This was what he'd dreamed of and what every alpha wanted.

She cried out in pleasure, her teeth sinking into his flesh. Triumph and pleasure tore through him as she marked him as her own.

He roared as he came in hard, fast pulses, buried deep inside her welcoming heat. His knot expanded quicker than ever before, locking them together.

His legs shook as he turned them and leaned back against the wall with her cradled in his arms. Protected. Adored.

"My little flower," he whispered, nuzzling her hair, her face, any part of her he could reach as his change receded. "Mother of my children. You are a wonder."

She stirred, lifting her head to smile up at him.

"You're pretty wonderful yourself. But... mother? At my age? That's not really likely to happen. Is it?"

"You don't know a lot about us. Do you? Once bonded, omegas share their alphas' lifespans." His smile was wicked as he lifted a hand to his bleeding neck. The wound would heal in hours, leaving a scar. Her mark. "And you just bonded yourself to me."

"I did? We are? Wait. So you're telling me that you and I..."

"Will be together for many years, my flower." He kissed her cheek. "And we will find our daughter, too."

"Ours?"

"Ours. We are bonded. She is family." He pulled back to look at her, his eyes dark with heat. "And you will give me children. Lots of them."

Her lips curved in a smile. "Is that so? When do you plan on that happening?"

He pushed away from the wall and walked toward the bedroom. "We're starting right now."

14

Leia pressed herself in tightly to Var's side and kept reminding herself to breathe. The low rumble of his parth was the only thing keeping her grounded at the moment, the steady sound dulling the edge of her fear.

She was surrounded by alphas. Not just any alphas, either. These were the Lord Overseer's most trusted men, and they were all looking at her. She tried not to think about it. If she did, the need to run tried to overwhelm her.

"My lord," Var rumbled, his arm around her shoulders. "This is my omega, Leia. Leia... this is Lord Tane, Overseer of Earth."

"My lord," she said softly, her eyes on the ground in front of her.

She'd seen him in the hallway during the attack, but this was different. This was her formal introduction to the alien who ruled her planet, and despite all Var's attempts to convince her that they were different than the L'crav, she still had her doubts.

"You may look at me, Leia." Tane's voice was cultured and surprisingly mild.

She heard murmurs from some of the others present, but no one spoke out.

Still, she kept her head down until Var squeezed her shoulders. "It's alright, little flower."

She looked up and found herself caught in the gaze of a predator.

"I..." Her words failed her.

The lord smiled, the expression softening his features a little. "I would talk to you, little omega. That will be impossible if you are terrified. I wish you no harm, nor would I see any omega brought to harm."

"You wouldn't?" She chewed on her lip for a moment and then summoned up her courage. "Then why did your people do this to us?"

Var tensed, but Tane smiled at her. "Incredible. You were right, my shield. She is not like the others."

Leia suppressed the urge to roll her eyes. Of

course she wasn't. And many of the others weren't the way they seemed either. It was the only way they'd been able to survive.

Tane tipped his head and looked at her, his eyes disconcertingly intense. "My people need omegas to survive. Normally, this happens differently. Your species, though." He shook his head. "Something new occurred here. That the L'crav couldn't see it is regrettable. Now that I am here, things will change."

She watched him for long moments and then flicked a glance toward Var. His closeness bolstered her courage.

"You changed us," she said bluntly. "We did not want to change. Many died. The rest..." She shrugged. "We have long memories and some will not forgive you. Ever."

A single muscle jumped in Tane's jaw, the only visible sign of his irritation, but she saw it. This was a man not used to being challenged. It was a failing of every Tolath she'd come across.

"What's done is done. You are changed. We are here and we are not leaving. Forgiveness is a luxury your species cannot afford. If the omegas come out of hiding, it will be better for them. Safer."

She didn't break eye contact. "You mean it will be better for you." It wasn't a question. It was a statement. "With all due respect, *my lord,* a warning. Forgiveness might well be a luxury we cannot afford, but vengeance is a currency we understand all too well."

Var's grip shifted and he stepped forward, trying to pull her behind him. "I'm sorry, my lord. I did warn you she was not like the others."

Tane raised a hand. "You did. And I am not done speaking with her. She is free to speak her mind before me. *For now.*"

Var glanced back at her, a warning in his eyes. "As you will, my lord."

Leia moved out from behind him. "What do you want to know?"

"The location of the omegas would be nice," Tane drawled. "But I doubt you're going to offer up that information. Are you?"

She shook her head. No way would she ever give up another omega. Var had turned out to be different, but she couldn't be sure about the rest of them. She would not doom another woman to a living hell.

Tane nodded. "Very well. Then instead, I have a question for you. What would it take to make you humans choose a currency other than vengeance? There is honor in that path, but blood and death lie at the end. There is no way you can prevail against us in any kind of battle. That has already been proven."

She shrugged. "Did I say anything about a battle? Fighting back would be revenge. Vengeance would be removing the one thing you need here more than anything."

Shocked murmurs filled the room. Var looked down at her with horror. "No."

"What do you think has been happening here for the last twenty years?" she asked, her voice hard with grief and the weight of dark memories. So many lives. Too many friends.

Tane growled. "This stops. *Now*."

She laughed, the sound bitter. "You can't stop us. It's our final choice. Our last moment of freedom. The Tolath took everything else away from us, but they can't take away that."

"But... that's not what's best for my people or yours." Tane's voice was low and horrified.

"What's *best* for my people was for yours to have flown right past us." Her words were blunt and cutting. "What would be best for us now would be for you to leave or just leave us alone. But you're not going to do that. Are you?" She didn't wait for him to answer. "You really want to know how to make things better? Then you need to show the omegas you're not abusive assholes who just want to fuck and breed them. Anything less, and you can wait for hell to freeze over before any of us will come to you willingly."

"*You* came," another alpha spoke up. "According to Var, you did it of your own free will."

She swallowed hard. *Savannah.* Var still hadn't found her.

"I bargained the only thing I had left in order to find my daughter—an omega who was taken by force. I thought maybe I could see her again before I died. I never imagined Var would show me any kindness." She looked up at him and smiled. "I never knew an alpha like him could exist. If you want to make things better. Be like Var. Protect us. Don't use us anymore."

Tane inclined his head. "I will take your advice under consideration."

"What? This is preposterous!" a deep voice exclaimed behind him. "They are omegas! They will submit! It is in their nature."

Var chuckled and pulled her back against him. His lips grazed her temple but before he could speak, she did.

"And that, whoever the hell you are, is why

you've all had blue balls for years."

The alpha growled. Var snarled back, and Tane threw out a hand. "Enough, General D'warr. As you can see, these omegas are different. I would not call this female submissive. I begin to see the problems the L'crav faced and why they failed so utterly. We will not fail." He shot a hard look at his men. "This is *our* world. These are *our* omegas. They are out there, and we *will* find them. We will protect them."

He nodded the slightest bit to Leia. "And thus we give them another choice."

It was more than she'd expected, the smallest tendril of hope unfurling in her chest as she looked up at Var with a smile. The love and admiration in his darkened eyes made warmth spiral through her.

The moment was shattered by a woman's cry and they all turned to see an alpha walk by the open hall door, a struggling woman over his broad shoulder. Because Var was in the way, she didn't get more than a vague impression.

"Starting with that one." Tane sighed, rubbing a hand over his face. "Someone find out what the xarth A'rath is doing with that female."

Var chuckled. "To me, little flower."

She turned and wrapped her arms around his neck obediently. He lifted her into his arms, cradling her against the solid bulk of his chest. "If you would excuse me, my lord. I need to take my omega to our rooms. I will return once I have seen to her comfort."

Tane nodded. "Dismissed. And Var?"

"Yes, my lord?"

"I will want my shield back at my side tomorrow. We have work to do."

"Yes, my lord." Var bowed his head and swept out of the room with her cradled against his chest.

"I'm going to have to punish you for what you did in there," he growled at her.

"I know. But it was worth it."

She leaned in and kissed him, unrepentant and happier than she could have ever imagined she'd be. It wasn't the deal she'd been expecting to make. It was so much better.

She'd traded her life away and received the promise of a lifetime of love with her alpha in return.

Thank you for reading Var and Leia's story. If you want to know what happens to Leia's daughter, Savannah... keep reading for a sneak peek at the next book - Rath.

BONUS CONTENT - RATH

There was food. It was half hidden in the ruins of a building, but it was there. She could smell it.

Savannah bit her lip as she hid in the shadows of a building opposite and watched the unguarded pack. Night had fallen, which was the only reason she'd crept this close with every instinct on alert. An alpha was in the area, but he was noisy and easy to avoid. As were the obvious traps he'd laid for her before—some sort of meat cooking over an open fire, left unattended, or cakes left next to an open pack.

She snorted at the memory. He must have thought she was stupid if he thought she couldn't spot such an obvious trap. Her mother had drilled it into her from a young age that omegas stayed hidden, always. Being an omega herself, Leia had taught

Savannah how to hide, even when nearly in plain sight, how to use the shadows to her advantage and... her hand moved down to touch the mercy on her thigh... and she'd picked up how to fight if necessary along the way. Not that an omega had much chance against an alpha. The most they could hope for was to trigger the beast and end up dead in the aftermath. If not... that's why the blade was called a mercy.

So she stayed motionless as she watched the backpack. She'd already been here an hour and she was prepared to stay in place a couple more, just to make sure that the pack she watched was not one of the traps laid out for her. She didn't think so, but it was better to stay hungry and wait than to move too soon and lose the only thing she had left.

Her freedom.

She'd already lost that once. The Lord Overseer's messengers had announced the ban on the claiming of omegas. That had been a trap, too—a lie sent out to lure the women out of hiding. Savanna hadn't believed it for a second, but others had. Another omega had been in the town center when she'd gone for water. She should have known better. She should have turned back the moment she saw her. One omega might slip past the alpha's sense of smell but two together was too much, especially when they were low on scent-blockers. If she had listened to what her mother had taught her and turned back, she wouldn't have been taken, but they needed the water. So she'd decided the risk was worth taking.

She'd been wrong.

Her recollections of the raid were little more than scattered fragments. Terror. Panic. The roar of the alphas. The screams. Something heavy had thumped against the side of her head and everything went dark.

That blow saved her. Unconscious for the journey to the alpha's outpost, she must have been out cold when they'd come to claim the others. Their terrified screams as they were claimed and knotted by one alpha after another had woken her. Dazed and unsteady, instinct had still kicked in and she'd crawled back into the shadows to hide. The building they'd been kept in was a ruined factory with plenty of hidey-holes. And, wonder of wonders, a way out. She hadn't believed it as her heart pounded in her chest, but she'd managed to wriggle through the tiny gap into the outside world, tearing her leg on something in the process.

Then she ran.

That had been almost a week ago. Maybe. The

wound in her leg had steadily gotten worse, and she'd lost track of the days. Now it was a dull, steady throb that threatened to overwhelm her. If she didn't eat something and get help soon...

She shoved the thought from her mind and focused on her goal. The pack. Food. Then she could work out her next move.

She didn't move until darkness had fallen completely. She remained still for another half hour, eyes wide and ears peeled for any signs of movement. The alpha that had claimed this section of an old ruined city had been moving around earlier this afternoon, but he'd kept to the paths he'd cleared. As long as she avoided those, she should be good.

Waiting until the moon disappeared behind the clouds, she slid from cover and darted across the gap to her objective. Her heart pounded in her ears. At any moment she expected a roar to fill the air and to be grabbed from behind.

It didn't happen. The night was quiet, and she let herself breathe a sigh of relief as she crouched beside the pack. It was partially hidden. She tugged it out from beneath a bit of broken board slowly to avoid noise.

Her prize in her grasp, she retreated into the shadows again. Only when she was curled up inside a small space beneath a shattered wall did she open her treasure to see what she had found.

Her fingers touched unimaginable softness first, and she pulled out a blanket of thick, warm material that made her feel the cold even more. She wrapped it around her shoulders and burrowed deeper into the softness before returning her attention to the rest of contents.

Food! Nothing like the cakes or cooking meat she'd been tempted by before. These were field rations. The squares were sealed in some kind of foil she had to tear at with her teeth and fingers. Once it was opened, she crammed a bit of the soft cake into her mouth and moaned. She didn't know what it tasted like and she didn't care. It was *food*.

A canteen lay at the bottom of the pack and she pulled it out while still chewing. She pried the lid off and held it in both hands, sniffing at the contents. Water. She took a sip to confirm that it was untainted and then drank half the container in long, greedy swallows. Her stomach cramped and she forced herself to stop drinking. Too much and she'd throw it back up. She couldn't afford to do that.

Carefully, she tightened the lid back on the canteen and put it back in the pack. She did the same with the unfinished ration, sealing it up in the foil as best she could before putting that away as well. Making sure the blanket was wrapped securely, she looped her arms through the backpack in case she had to run. She wasn't leaving it behind. It was the only way she had to survive.

Knees drawn up, she rested her cheek on the top of the pack and closed her eyes. Already she could feel the shivers setting in. The wound on her leg wasn't right. She knew that, but she'd been through this kind of thing before. She would survive or she wouldn't. That wasn't her decision to make. All she could do was focus on what she could control. And right now, that meant sleep. A couple of hours was all she needed, and then she would move again.

Her eyes fluttered closed finally and she drifted off...

Ready for more? Find Rath and the rest of the Omega Collective series at alienalphas.com and be sure to Join the Omega Collective newsletter for exclusive news and series updates.

ABOUT THE AUTHORS

Mina Carter

Author, photographer and cover artist, Mina Carter can usually be found hunched over a keyboard or behind a camera, frantically trying to get the images and words in her head out and onto the screen before they drive her mad. She was addicted to coffee and chocolate, but unfortunately both now dislike her. Want to know more about Mina's books?

Check out her website: Minacarter.com

Susan Hayes

Susan lives on Vancouver Island off the Canadian west coast where the waters are patrolled by orcas and the sighting of snowflakes leads to citywide panic. She's jumped out of perfectly good airplanes on purpose and accidentally swum with sharks on the Great Barrier Reef.

If the world ends, she plans to survive as the

spunky, comedic sidekick to the heroes of the new world, because she's too short and out of shape to make it on her own for long. Want to know more about Susan's books?

Check out her website: Susanhayes.ca

Made in the USA
Monee, IL
30 July 2021